THE WRETCHED TAIL

BY
SARI ANN KOEHLER

Sari Ann Koehler (signature)

The Wretched Tail

Copyright ©2015 Sari Ann Koehler

I dedicate this story to:
My first road trip buddies~ Alex and Chase;
The cats that helped my writing process ~
Wendall, Sox, Mr. Kitten, Frickie, and Tippy;
and my best critics~
Alex, Presli, Camri, Mom, Broc, Bonnie, and Chase.

Here's to good times, good trips, and dueling
banjos.

Table of Contents

Chapter 1	The Fight	1
Chapter 2	Timber	4
Chapter 3	The Cornfield	8
Chapter 4	The Quest	12
Chapter 5	Predicaments	17
Chapter 6	Uncle Tom	21
Chapter 7	The Journey	26
Chapter 8	Rule of Tongue	30
Chapter 9	Agony	36
Chapter 10	Letters	41
Chapter 11	Billie	48
Chapter 12	The Cave	55
Chapter 13	Sacrifice	63
Chapter 14	The Meal	68
Chapter 15	Caprihorn, Tilo, and Prong	73
Chapter 16	Hard-Hearted	80
Chapter 17	Miss Muffet	85
Chapter 18	The Storm	90
Chapter 19	Wreckage	93
Chapter 20	Better Off	99
Chapter 21	Safe	104
Chapter 22	Rejection	107
Chapter 23	Cloudy Flatcars	112
Chapter 24	Dust	117
Chapter 25	Friends	124
Chapter 26	Silver Heart	128

Chapter 27   Perfect Stranger   133
Chapter 28   Bwack Wiwwow   140
Chapter 29   Bonded Promise   146
Chapter 30   Unselfish Love   152
Chapter 31   Compassion and Love   157
Chapter 32   Sick   163
Chapter 33   Loss   168
Chapter 34   Torture   175
Chapter 35   Tarnished   183
              Epilogue   191

CHAPTER ONE
THE FIGHT

"Here, kitty, kitty," Dusti taunted.

A young ginger tabby cat and an old Himalayan huddled together by a cottonwood tree. A long gash slid across the tabby's face. Blood matted the Himalayan's white fur.

A tan Savannah cat crept across the cottonwood's branches. His black cheetah spots wove through the leaves. His large black pupils dilated, hungrily devouring anything that got in his way. He twitched his hips back and forth as if winding himself up.

Dusti ran for the tabby and Himalayan. He arced his back and hissed as if claiming the two scared cats as his prey.

The heavy Savannah dove out of the tree, tackling Dusti to the ground. His front claws ripped across Dusti's cheek. His back claws tore down Dusti's spine, catching on his spiraled tail.

Dusti grabbed the Savannah, wrapping his clawless forepaws around the Savannah's haunches. He threw the large Savannah away from the cottonwood as if he was merely a toy ball.

Dusti stood, balancing on the tips of his back paws. He smiled, resting his protruding bottom tooth on his muzzle. "Go home, Savannah. They're mine."

A long intimidating hiss pelted out of the Savannah's mouth.

The Himalayan and tabby cowered as if trying to disappear.

Dusti sat on his back haunches like a sentry before the two scared cats, his broad chest barring the Savannah's way.

The Savannah withered into a pouncing stance.

Dusti would not move.

The Savannah dropped his head below his shoulders and slunk away.

Dusti cringed as he stood up and flexed his back. He glanced at the Himalayan and tabby.

Harsh wind beat against the Himalayan's feeble body. Fur spiked out sporadically around his smashed in muzzle. A tuft of gray fur curled in a cowlick above his round blue eyes.

Dusti twitched his mouth, hiding a smile tugging at his whiskers. The old cat had seen better days.

"I don't want to fight you, Bushy," Dusti said.

"My name is not Bushy," the Himalayan said. "I am the Great Tippy-Tippy Roo-Roo."

"Sure, Bushy."

Tippy paced back and forth on the cracked dirt. He

sniffed the thick air and held his head against the hot, heavy wind. He pointed his paw at the dry cottonwood leaves. "Do you see that? The earth is changing. Do you feel it?"

Dusti shrugged.

Tippy's eyes bore through Dusti. "The air is harsh and bitter. It is dry where it needs water. And wet where it needs earth. Through time they have said that a Bobtailed Manx would come with a short tail that spiraled tightly. He would fight off the bad and protect the good, but sympathize with them both. You are that Bobtailed Manx."

Dusti shook his head and walked away from the Himalayan.

Tippy ran after Dusti and batted his curled tail. "Bloodlines run deep. Your tail gives you away. It kinks just like a Japanese Bobtail, but your broad chest bears the bloodlines of Manx. You are a Bobtailed Manx."

Tippy ran toward the tree. "The United States is changing. The time has come."

"For what?"

"Are you ready?"

"For what?"

Tippy jumped in the air and ran up the cottonwood's trunk defying gravity. "I will see you soon. You are the one."

Tippy hurdled over the lowest limb and vanished as his paws hit the tree's rough bark.

CHAPTER TWO
TIMBER

"Whoa," the ginger tabby said. "That was weird."

Dusti searched for a hole around the limbs of the wide cottonwood. "Where did he go?"

"He disappeared," the tabby said.

Dusti shook his head. He rested his grayish brown paws on the rough bark and scanned up the tree. "There must be a hole or something he jumped into." He squinted at the point where Tippy had vanished.

"No, he disappeared." The tabby rubbed her paw on Dusti's back.

Dusti shrugged it off. "Why didn't you disappear, too, Ginger?"

"The name's Timber and I don't know how to disappear." She licked her paw and scrubbed the cut on her face. "Do you have a name or should I call you *the one*?""

"My name's Dusti."

"What did Tippy mean when he said *you are the one*?"

"You know as much as I do," Dusti said. "He's just a

crazy old cat."

Dusti walked away from the tree, down the long dirt road.

The bright orange sun rested on Colorado's Uncompahgre Plateau bathing the sky in fire.

"I don't think Tippy's crazy," Timber said matter-of-factly. "But I'm not staying by that tree. It gives me the willies, too. Why does your tail curl like that?"

"I was born that way." Dusti scurried down the dirt road, toward the corn shed. He dove into the dry sagebrush gating the roadside, hoping to lose Timber. He wove through the acrid sage, stirring the dusty leaves to cover his scent.

Timber sprang in front of Dusti. "Your tail's cute. I love how it spirals. Can you straighten it?"

"Nope. It's kinked."

"I wish mine was kinked. I bet it never gets in the way. How come your jaw's crooked?"

Dusti slid his protruding bottom tooth off of his muzzle and raced through the sagebrush.

Tall semis guarded a corn shed across the road. The wind blew a deep green scent of fresh picked corn off a farm next door.

Dusti darted into the farm and zigzagged across the bare ground.

White chalky alkali covered the farm's empty fields. The dry adobe soil cracked in the heat and drought of the season.

Corn stalks waved from one lonely field as a long gated

pipe stretched across the front of the cornfield.

Timber jumped onto the gated pipe. "You're pretty fast, but you can't get rid of me that easy."

"Why don't you go home?" Dusti asked.

"I can't. I'm a stray and always have been. Unlike you, spoiled, pampered kitties, I don't live in a mansion, house, or even a shack, or barn. I don't get tuna and milk for dinner. Some of us cats aren't that lucky."

"I don't have a home either." Dusti stared at the purple peaks of the San Juan Mountains stretching across the southern horizon. "I used to, but don't anymore."

"What happened? Were you too young and wild to let a family hold you back?"

"Both of us can obviously survive on our own. Please, go away."

"I can't survive. You saved my life. Now I have to return the favor."

"The Savannah would have roughed you up a bit, but he wouldn't have killed you. He was a pansy."

"I still owe you and Tippy, too. If Tippy hadn't appeared out of the tree when he did, the Savannah would have ripped me to shreds. And if you hadn't come when you did, Tippy would have been a goner."

"You owe Tippy, then, not me. Pay him back."

"I can't. Tippy disappeared. Remember. I can't follow him, but you're easy to follow. If I pay you back, Tippy will owe me and I owe Tippy, so everything will be even."

Dusti closed his eyes. He inhaled a deep breath, letting the relaxing smell of earth weave into his body. He slowly opened his eyes.

"Peek-a-boo," Timber said. "I'm still here."

"You're not leaving?"

"Nope," Timber said.

Dusti rounded his paw toward the cornfield. "Okay. This is where I live."

"In a cornfield?"

"Yeah, where do you live?"

"In a cornfield now."

CHAPTER THREE
THE CORNFIELD

A full gibbous moon hung between twinkling stars when Dusti stretched awake from his cat nap and leaped over the gated pipe. He walked down a furrow into the center of the cornfield.

Corn stalks covered the moonlight, casting an eerie darkness across the field. Ears of forgotten corn pointed from the middle of the stalks.

Dusti jumped onto a corn stalk and grabbed an ear of corn. As it fell he let go, landing on his paws.

He nudged the ear to Timber. "Eat up."

Dusti sprang again onto a corn stalk and batted another ear down. He wove his paw under the green sheath of corn, tearing off the sheets of green and corn silk with his teeth.

Sweet, sugary corn juice squirted into his mouth as he bit into the crunchy golden kernels.

Bits of corn stuck to Timber's muzzle after she finished eating.

"You're supposed to eat your food," Dusti said, "not

wear it."

"That's pretty big talk," Timber said, "coming from a cat with corn on his whiskers and corn on his nose. Tell me, will you grow corn wherever you go?"

Dusti ducked behind a corn stalk. He quickly licked his lips, tasting the unwelcome sugary corn juice. He shook his head, berating himself for calling out Timber.

Small corn kernels pattered off of his whiskers and onto the ground.

Dusti growled. He mopped the dust from his paws and washed his face. He twisted around to wash the cut on his spine, but the skin pulled apart as if horrid claws were tearing the cut wider.

"Wait, Dusti," Timber said, slipping around the corn stalk. "Let me help."

Dusti tensed as Timber's soft wet paw slid down his back.

"Relax," Timber said. "This wound won't get better unless it's cleaned."

Dusti cringed as Timber's rough tongue bathed his back. It grated against the scratch as she went over it again and again.

Dusti's eyes grew heavy as Timber's warm tongue combed through his fur. A quiet purr gurgled from his throat. His paws couldn't support him anymore. He sank to the ground.

Timber licked the scratch on Dusti's face. She rubbed her nose along his muzzle.

Dusti ripped his eyes open. "What was that?"

Timber giggled. "A noodgie, you know a cat kiss."

"I know what a noodgie is," Dusti said. "Why did you give it to me?"

"You were purring."

"You cleaned my wounds. You've paid me back. You need to go."

"Where am I supposed to go? Down a couple of furrows. Forget it. I'm not going anywhere."

Dusti batted the corn cob Timber had been eating. "If you insist on staying, there needs to be a few rules, no noodgies, no cuddles, and no kneading. I'm a cat that needs to be alone."

"But doesn't like to be alone."

"You don't know what I like. You don't know anything about me."

"Because you won't tell me."

Dusti scowled at his front paws. Tears burned his eyes. He blinked them back before Timber could see. "Some things are better forgotten."

"How can they be forgotten if it still causes you pain?"

"Do you want to stay?"

"I have to until I pay you back."

"Then drop it."

Dusti turned his back and lay on the hard adobe ground.

Crickets chirped as the wind ruffled through the tall corn stalks. Dusti had to get rid of Timber. He could not get close to her.

After a few restless catnaps, Dusti jerked wide awake as

Timber's slumbered breathing grew heavier. If he wanted to lose her, he had to do it now.

Creeping over to the corn stalks guarding the next furrow, he shifted silently through them and crawled towards the gated pipe.

He twisted his ears. The corn stalks swished back and forth.

The smell of animal fur hung in the air.

Dusti darted between the next two corn stalks.

Four little feet pattered across his paw as a field mouse scurried into the next furrow.

Dusti sighed and crept out of the field. He looked behind him.

The labyrinth of corn stalks swayed as the wind blew southward off Grand Mesa.

No one was there. Timber hadn't seen him or followed.

Dusti squinted at the gated pipe.

A bushy white cat sat on top of it, pushing one of the black gates shut. The wind blew against his frail body.

"Tippy," Dusti muttered and turned back towards the field.

"I would not go back in there," Tippy said.

"I can see you. I can see all things, Dusti."

CHAPTER FOUR
THE QUEST

"How do you know my name?" Dusti asked.

"I know all things," Tippy said. He sat on the gated pipe. His pale blue eyes burned through Dusti's body into his soul. "Are you ready?"

"For what? I don't know all things like you, Tippy-Tippy Roo-Roo."

Tippy blew out the side of his mouth. His gray cowlick fluttered. A long silver tear leaked out of his eye. "The United States is changing, Dusti. It is imbalanced. It is wet where it needs earth and dry where it needs water. Disasters rage across the United States because of the imbalance. As disasters toll, they hurt and kill all living things. The United States is dying, taking all of us with it."

The corn stalks rustled as Tippy sat balanced on the pipe. His silver tears pooled on the ground.

"Throughout time towns, cities, and societies have been on the brink of disaster," Tippy said, "and destroyed because the elements remained imbalanced."

Dusti scooped up a paw full of dirt. "This isn't a disaster. It's only a drought. Tell your disaster saga to someone else, Tippy-Tippy Roo-Roo. I don't believe it. No cities or societies have ever been destroyed."

"What about Atlantis?" Tippy asked.

Dusti jumped over the pipe. "Purely myth."

"Only to skeptics. The Minoans, however, did come to ruin after the Thera volcano exploded around 1500 B.C. And in 1883 the Krakatau Volcano exploded creating huge tsunamis. Two hundred ninety-five towns were destroyed in Java and Sumatra Indonesia. Countless lives of people, animals, and plants were taken by this disaster."

"Volcanoes and tsunamis are natural disasters," Dusti said walking down the road.

"And what's a drought?"

Dusti jerked to a stop.

Tippy's white fur haloed his feeble body in an iridescent glow. His paws held firmly to the gated pipe. "Dusti, I come to you because you are the one. Will you heed the call?"

"What call?"

"You have to save the United States and all of us."

Dusti closed his eyes. He cringed as an image of Ryan, the human boy he used to take care of, bombarded his mind. He could never forget Ryan's silent tears or the deep black-purple bruises spotting his body and circling his baby blue eyes. "You have the wrong cat, I can't even save one little boy, let alone countless people and animals."

"Yes, you can. Saving is in your soul."

Dusti stared at the ground.

Tippy jumped off the pipe. "You saved Timber and me yesterday."

Dusti shook his head.

Tippy's coarse paw lifted Dusti's chin. His sparkly blue eyes stared into Dusti's. "You saved Ryan in more ways than you know, can't you save him one more time?"

A shiver ran through Dusti's body. "How do you know about Ryan?"

"I told you, I know all things."

Dusti squinted at Tippy. "How can I save the United States? I can't stop natural disasters. I can warn humans of pending disasters, but they won't listen. Animal warnings are only marveled at after disasters strike, they're never considered before."

"You're making this too complicated. All I ask of you is to balance the United States."

"How?"

"You will start by giving the Pigsie Fairies something they have needed for a while."

Dusti closed his eyes. Pigsie Fairies? This old cat was insane. Fairies didn't exist.

Tippy darted to the gated pipe and grated a black gate open. He reached in, pulling out a small gold cardboard box with a baby blue lid and orange twine tied around it. Holding the twine in his teeth, he sat it on the ground before Dusti.

"Where's Timber?" Tippy asked.

"She's asleep."

Tippy's eye twitched almost in a wink. "Good, good. She could not handle going on this quest. It would cause her unspeakable pain."

Tippy's eyes pulsated. His chaotic fur bushed around his head in every direction. "This will not be an easy quest for you either. It will put your life in utter peril. You will see things you never want to see and hope to never see again."

"Like Pigsie Fairies?"

"Before the United States gets better, Mr. Skeptic, it will only get worse. I need your solemn vow that no matter what happens, no matter what is taken from you, no matter what you see, you will finish this quest and return to me."

Dusti sank to the ground. He held his paws on his forehead, trying to unravel everything Tippy had said.

It felt as if a freight train had blown through his head spilling too much information.

Dusti closed his eyes, wiping his thoughts clean.

A small freckled face Ryan danced across his mind. A huge smile lit up his face as he cuddled and petted Dusti on his lap.

If Tippy knew all things, maybe he knew where Ryan lived now. If Dusti could help save Ryan one more time, maybe Ryan would take him back.

Dusti stared into Tippy's baby blue eyes. "I'll return on one condition, Tippy. When I complete this quest you have to tell me where Ryan is."

Tippy nodded. "Of course, I wouldn't have it any other way." He nudged the small box over to Dusti. "This box contains one of earth's most precious commodities. Protect this box with your life. Don't open it. Give this box to the Pigsie Fairies. It will start reversing the hands of fate. Start on your journey now, before the sun rises, or it will be too late."

"Where are the Pigsie Fairies?" Dusti asked.

"They are where the pronghorns and mountain goats roam. Trust in yourself and other creatures, Dusti. Only then will you find the Pigsie Fairies' home."

"How do I get there?"

Tippy ran toward the gated pipe. "Go to a place where corn is stored, find a Tom's Reefer and climb on board. Many miles and hours will pass as you ride. Get out when letters glow on a hillside."

Dusti stared at the small gold cardboard box, hammering Tippy's riddle into his memory. He looked towards the corn shed and then at the slowly fading purple predawn haze. "What's a reefer?"

Silence crashed around Dusti. He squinted at the gated pipe. Tippy was no longer there.

CHAPTER FIVE
PREDICAMENTS

Dusti tore across the corn shed's graveled parking lot. He held the gold box's twine tightly in his teeth. It felt warm like cat's breath as it bumped against his jaw.

Dusti glanced east toward the rising sun. A pink tinge glowed on the rim of the Black Canyon. He had to find a reefer and tom before it was too late.

Diesel fumes sliced through the pink morning sunrise. The ground shuddered as a group of semis roared to life.

White, crimson, maroon, and pine-green semis stretched out in a row. The green semi pulled a long flat trailer that stretched out like a reef, while the white, maroon, and crimson semis pulled large boxed trailers.

Semis could go many miles for many hours. A reefer must be a semi.

Dusti crept between the white and crimson semis.

A young skinny man sat in the driver's seat of the white semi's cab. His knuckles glared deathly white as he gripped the steering wheel. His mouth moved silently and he nodded as if giving himself a pep talk.

Dusti backed away from the white cab. The poor kid didn't look like he could handle driving a big rig, let alone driving with a stow away cat.

A sallow faced truck driver wearing a loose red shirt sat in the crimson's cab. Long black hair fell down the truck driver's back and framed her face in a girly hairstyle.

A lady truck driver definitely wasn't a tom.

Two down two to go.

Dusti laughed at himself as he walked around the crimson semi. He was so gullible, putting his faith in a crazy old cat.

But somehow Tippy had known he would do anything to save Ryan. Even if that meant riding a big rig with a stranger, searching for mystical beings that didn't exist, balancing the United States with a twine tied cardboard box.

Dusti shook his head as he crawled behind the maroon semi. This quest was insane and would never work, but at least it got him away, soon to be far away, from Timber.

A blast of cold air barreled out of the maroon semi's open trailer doors. Boxes piled on top of each other in the refrigerated trailer.

Reefer . . . Refrigerated.

Dusti scurried in front of the maroon semi's trailer. He hid behind its front tire as a curly, honey blonde haired man stood on the cab's footstep.

A huge boxed fan spun on the front of the maroon semi's trailer making a choppy sound like train wheels on a railroad track. Condensation dripped down the mud flaps and made a small puddle on the ground.

The curly haired man reached through the cab's open window. He jumped off the semi's footstep holding a stack of papers and walked to the corn shed's office.

Dusti clenched the box's twine in his teeth and jumped, flying through the open window.

The chair gasped as his paws landed on the soft cushioned captain seat.

Twenty circular gages cascaded across the dash. A long black stick shift sat between two gray captain seats with a black curvy CB cord jostling above it.

A long gray curtain hung halfway between the driver and passenger seats, separating the sleeper section of the cab from the driver's section.

Dusti batted the cord and ran between the seats into the sleeper section of the semi.

Green cotton sheets stretched across a pulled out sofa bed. A small black refrigerator hummed in front of the sofa bed on the passenger side.

Dusti ducked underneath the sofa bed, hiding perfectly in a square cubbyhole.

Diesel, salt, and a faint scent of sulfur exuded from a pair of boots under the bed.

Dropping the box, Dusti curled his top lip around his nose and opened his mouth. He had smelled that same exact scent before when he lived with Ryan.

"ROOW."

Dusti's ears pricked. He sprang into the driver's seat. Timber's front paws bent over the open window as she clung to the door.

"What are you doing?" Dusti yelled.

"You need me," Timber said.

"No, I don't. Tippy told me this journey would be too hard on you."

Timber's haunches rose as her back paws crept farther up the door. "I heard everything Tippy said. 'It would cause her unspeakable pain.' You boys are all the same. You want to save the world by yourself, so you can get all the glory in the end.

"Too bad Dusti, I'm saving the United States right along with you. You need me." Her back paws climbed onto the windowsill. Her body swayed as she tried to gain balance.

Dusti leaped on his back paws and pushed Timber off the windowsill.

Flying through the air, Timber turned her body and kicked the door with her hind paws. She cleared the foot-step, landing like a gymnast on the gravel ground.

Dusti peered out the window. "Sorry, Timber."

"Not as sorry as you're going to be." She hopped on the footstep. "ROOW," she cried.

Dusti crawled behind the passenger seat. He watched the driver's door, covering his ears as Timber's incessant cries grew monotonously worse.

CHAPTER SIX
UNCLE TOM

Daylight glimmered above the cliffs of the Black Canyon. The semi door clicked open, ceasing Timber's loud cry. A piney smell of soap, aftershave, and deodorant crowded the cab.

The curly blonde haired man hopped into the semi. His tan arm ran back and forth as he leaned out the door and petted what Dusti could only suspect was Timber.

"Mew," Timber said hopping into the cab. She rubbed the side of her mouth on the man's outstretched fingers. She kneaded his lap, flexing her orange paws back and forth.

The man chuckled and stroked Timber's back. He wove his hand underneath her stomach and tried to pull her off, but Timber's claws clung to his blue jeans.

"Kitty," the man said. He spoke in a low voice as if apologizing. He wagged Timber back and forth, prying her sharp claws out of his jeans.

"Good," Dusti said as the man set Timber outside.

"Now start driving."

"ROOW," Timber cried.

"Ignore the cat," Dusti said.

The man's shoulders sagged over the steering wheel. Tears pooled in his wide, baby blue eyes. He shook his head as if berating himself and opened the door. "Here, kitty, kitty."

Timber leaped onto the man's lap before he could think twice. A purr as loud as a chainsaw clattered from her throat.

The man spoke soothingly to Timber. He set her like a princess on the passenger seat.

A seat belt clicked. The man pulled a yellow lever on the bottom middle of the dash and rolled the semi away from the corn shed. The semi rumbled onto the main road heading north toward the Grand Mesa.

Dusti crept behind the boots and rested his head on his folded paws. Timber would mess up everything. He had to get rid of her before she did.

Diesel, salt, and sulfur drifted from the boots and joined the smell of pine. They teased Dusti's nose as if trying to stir a memory.

The man's wide baby blue eyes glanced at Timber.

"Uncle Tom," Dusti whispered. His heart pounded. He scurried farther under the bed as far away from Uncle Tom as he could get in the confined cab.

The last time he had seen Uncle Tom was when he lived in the huge house with Ryan.

Brown, cardboard boxes had filled the huge house when Uncle Tom had come to visit. Ryan and his mom, Patricia, were just about to move with Ryan's stepdad, Burt.

Uncle Tom was upstairs when Burt slammed through the door carrying the sour scent of whiskey.

Burt staggered through the house, kicking boxes out of his way. His loud voice slurred words together. He stumbled downstairs heading straight for Ryan's bedroom.

Dusti darted into Ryan's room.

Ryan hid behind his bed. He hugged his knees to his chest. He bundled into a ball, making his ten-year old body as small as he could, almost invisible.

Dusti noodgied Ryan under his bruised cheek.

A loud crack banged through the hall. An empty box rolled past Ryan's door.

Dusti burst into the doorway. He arced his back and hissed.

Burt barreled through the door, not letting anything stand in his way.

Searing white-hot pain emanated from Dusti's jaw and coursed through his face as he stumbled sideways. He raced toward Ryan trying to stay ahead of Burt and ignore the pain.

The smell of diesel, salt, sulfur, and pine swept downstairs. Uncle Tom pounded into the hall like a herd of elephants. He grabbed the swaying Burt before he got to Ryan. Looping Burt's arm around his shoulder, Tom helped Burt upstairs while talking to him in a soothing voice.

Dusti and Ryan crept into the hall. Patricia leaned against the wall and scooted up into a standing position. She held her hand over her left shoulder. She ruffled Ryan's curly, blonde hair.

Ryan and Dusti stood in the stairway as Patricia met Uncle Tom on the stair's landing.

Uncle Tom grabbed Patricia's shoulders just under a welt forming on her arm. He yelled, shaking her brittle body, and pointed at the door. He threw his hand to where Ryan stood.

Tears welled up in Uncle Tom's wide, baby blue eyes. He spoke through gritted teeth and pounded his hand on his chest.

Patricia looked down at the floor and shook her head. The house shook as Uncle Tom yelled. He yanked open the front door and slammed it shut. Tires squealed in the driveway. Headlights flew down the road as Uncle Tom sped away.

Patricia crumpled against the door. Her body shook. Tears poured from her eyes.

Uncle Tom had hurt Patricia worse than Burt ever had. She had never cried like that no matter how much Burt had hurt her.

Dusti crawled out from under the bed. He clamped the Pigsie Fairies' box in his mouth and hopped silently onto the bed, just behind the curtain, giving him the perfect view of Timber, and out both sleeper windows.

Timber's face rested on top of her crossed orange paws.

Deep breaths stretched out her skinny tummy. Her whiskers twitched as the tip of her tail tickled her orange heart shaped nose.

Dusti grimaced. He needed to get Timber away from Tom as soon as possible. He'd never let Tom hurt another innocent person or cat.

CHAPTER SEVEN
THE JOURNEY

Rugged canyon walls guarded the roadside as the semi sped down a four lane road through De Beque Canyon. A collage of crimson, yellow, and peach burned into the canyon as if fire and sunset had been fossilized into its walls.

Grand Mesa stood to the south of the canyon. A decaying gray crept in between patches of green clinging to the mountain begging for life. The flat topped mountain shrank against the horizon, pleading for rain.

The sun glared through the windshield as De Beque Canyon fell away into miles of coarse flat topped hills.

Tom flipped down his sun visor, revealing a picture of Ryan, Burt, and Patricia. Red straight pins poked through Burt, camouflaging his black tuxedo.

Dusti deeply inhaled the salt, sulfur, and diesel smell while looking at the picture, his only connections to his past.

He closed his eyes picturing Ryan's ten-year old face. He hoped Tippy's quest was real and not an intangible farce.

Stomach acid burned the edge of Dusti's throat as he looked out the left sleeper section's window.

A white car zipped past the semi on the left. Three children waved in the backseat, excitedly pulling their arms up and down.

A smile lit up Tom's face. He reached up and grabbed a leather rope next to the visor.

Dusti jumped as a blaring horn boomed throughout the cab. The horns tremor rattled his ear hair and echoed in his eardrums, slowly hammering away.

The semi soared down the road, climbing hills and turning with the greatest of ease as minutes dragged into hours.

Timber sat confidently in the passenger seat, grinning foolishly while looking out the window.

A noxious rotten egg odor oozed through the air vents as Glenwood Canyon's deep iron red walls bloomed around the semi.

The Colorado River snaked along the base of the canyon. Boulders slashed through the riverbed. A white streak lined the riverbed's crest like a bathtub ring. A stream wove around the boulders.

What once had been the majestic Colorado River was now only a stream.

Darkness ate the semi as if someone had turned off the sun.

Dusti's heart pounded in his ears. Was he too late? Had everything died?

Whistling bounded around the semi as it curved to the

left and then to the right in the darkness. Nothing could be seen out the windows, but a big wall of darkness that could smash the semi into crushed metal at anytime.

Dusti flattened his ears. He pinched his eyes shut. The quivering bed jarred his stomach. He swallowed the rancid corn and loud scream creeping up his throat.

Bright light teased his eyelids, but Dusti couldn't unglue them.

Kneading his front paws back and forth in the air, Dusti tried circulating the blood that had pooled in them. He rolled his head around his shoulders releasing the tension in his neck. He gulped down his queasy stomach, swallowed a huge breath of air, and pried his eyes open.

Hundreds of aspen trees crowded the roadside like one big family. Their long, white trunks quaked against the heavy wind blowing through Colorado's Rocky Mountains. Parched leaves held tight to the aspen's brittle limbs as if hoping water would soon come.

A gust of wind escaped the confines of aspens and roared across the road. The semi jerked to the left as the wind hit it like a bulldozer.

Dusti clenched onto the edge of the bed, trying to find his lost center of gravity. He ducked his head beneath his shoulders, cowering and cursing Tippy. Cats weren't meant to ride in vehicles. It demeaned them. Small and low to the ground was how Dusti preferred to get around.

Tom shifted the stick shift like a magic wand as the semi climbed hills and twisted along the road, passing small mining and ski towns.

Timber rode through the mountain hills, wind, and curves as if they were an enjoyable carnival ride. She meowed excitedly and patted the window when she saw anything interesting in the mountains.

Tom chuckled. He kept his eyes set like stone on the road and his hands gripped safely on the steering wheel as if reassuring an uninvited guest hiding in the sleeper section.

The air grew thinner the higher up the mountain the semi climbed.

Dusti's brain pounded against his skull. He inhaled deeply, but the thin absent air made him feel light headed.

Brown pine needles blanketed the Rocky Mountains as the semi wove around its curves. Brittle pine trees drooped as if their pine needles were too heavy to hold.

Dusti stared out the window. A tear leaked from his eye. The drought wasn't secluded to western Colorado, but had stretched its destruction for hundreds of miles throughout the state. What other states had the drought impacted? How far west or south had the drought's damage reached? How many thousands of miles in the United States were pleading for water?

Dusti cupped his front leg protectively around the gold box and cuddled next to it as if it was a security blanket. How did Tippy expect him to save the United States from drought with only one little box and limited instructions in riddle form? He couldn't do this. He had never saved anything form catastrophe.

All he had ever done was delay the inevitable.

CHAPTER EIGHT
RULE OF TONGUE

The semi slowed as Tom pulled onto an exit.

Dusti grabbed the gold box and hopped under the bed. He hid it securely behind Tom's boots where no one looking into the sleeper section would find it.

Pacing under the bed, his heart pounded throughout his body, ringing in his ears and tingling in his paws. If they stopped now he only had limited time to convince Timber of Tom's cruelty, get Timber out of the semi, and hide before Tom caught him.

Diesel fumes severed the air as Tom turned into a truck stop, maneuvering the semi to a rectangular metal fuel tank. The door clicked loudly open. A gust of miserably hot wind barreled into the semi.

"ROW?" Timber asked Tom.

"Kitty," Tom said. He gave Timber a reassuring pet and closed the semi's door.

"Timber," Dusti whispered as he ran in between the passenger seat. "You need to leave."

"Dusti?" Timber asked. "Here on the same exact semi

as me? What are the chances?"

"I know the truck driver, Tom," Dusti said. "He's a bad guy."

"You don't know Tom," Timber said. "He has been unbelievably nice to me, unlike you."

"Tom is the uncle of Ryan, the boy I adopted," Dusti said. "Tom abused Patricia, Ryan's mom."

"Tom hit Patricia?"

"No, Burt hit Patricia, but Tom yelled at her and made her cry."

"Oh wow. Call the pound. Tell me, Dusti, did he yell at her before or after Burt hit her."

"After, but that doesn't matter. Go before Tom hurts you."

Timber motioned out the windshield. Cars zipped down the busy roads. "I'm not getting out here so I can become roadkill. I can handle Tom yelling a lot better than a car running over me. Besides, Tippy wouldn't have had us ride with Tom if he was bad."

"Tippy wasn't planning on **us** riding with Tom. He was planning on **me** riding with him. Tippy knows all things. He knows I can handle an abusive guy like this."

"Since Tippy knows all things, he must have known I was hopping in the truck, too. I'm not going anywhere."

The driver's door grated open.

Dusti dove behind the curtain.

Tom climbed the semi's steps. He held a noose made out of orange twine in one hand and a water bottle in the other. He set the water bottle between the seats and reached over to Timber. He loosened the noose beside Timber's head.

Dusti glanced toward where the gold box was hidden and then at Timber.

Tom held the noose open with his forefinger and thumb of both hands.

"Please, Timber," Dusti pleaded silently. "Run away."

After a little prodding, Timber ducked through the noose.

Tom tightened the noose around Timber's neck. He held the twine in one hand, Timber in the other, and carried her out of the semi, towards the busy road.

Dusti hopped on the bed and hit the hot glass window. How was he supposed to save the United States when he couldn't even save one cat? Why did Tippy think he could do this?

Inhaling a long deep breath, he ran full force across the bed. He rolled into a ball, colliding against the left sleeper's window.

The cut on his spine ripped open.

The window wouldn't budge.

Dusti backed up. He felt as if smoke was flaring from his nostrils. He ran toward the window again.

Tom's silhouette appeared outside. He held a trail of orange twine taut in his hand.

A skinny ginger cat skipped through the gas station on the other end of the twine.

Dusti flung out his back claws. His front paws slid across the thin cotton sheets.

BOOM.   His head bashed against the window.

Dusti hopped off the bed and ducked underneath before Tom opened the door. He must have underestimated Timber if she could keep such a ruthless man from harming her.

Tom pulled the semi away from the diesel tanks and maneuvered into a parking lot next door. The aroma of greasy chicken exuded from a red barn-shaped building.

Brown liquid trickled onto the pavement as Tom dumped out a sixteen-ounce mug. He snatched the water bottle from between the seats and poured a long stream into the cup.

Dusti licked his dry, sand papery tongue as he watched the water flow out of the bottle.

Tom placed the mug in the cup holder closest to Timber. He cracked his window, patted Timber, and hopped out of the semi.

Timber plummeted into the back. "Are you okay?"

"Yeah, I'm fine. Are you?"

"Of course I'm fine, but you're not. Your cut is bleeding again. Here I'll clean it."

Dusti kneaded the floor as Timber's warm tongue swathed his back. "What did Tom do to you?"

"Nothing."

"He put a noose around your neck. I know he did something. Come on, Timber. You can tell me. You don't have to be ashamed."

"You're right. I don't have to be ashamed. Every cat does it. If you must know, Tom took me to the bathroom.

That's it."

"Why did he put the noose around your neck, then?"

"Probably so I wouldn't get excited, run towards the road, and become roadkill. Tom isn't a bad person, Dusti. He won't hurt me and he won't hurt you."

"Believe what you want, but I know the truth."

"Trust in other creatures, Dusti, isn't that what Tippy said?"

"Tippy didn't say anything about trusting humans."

"You're right, Dusti. Why trust Tom? He only takes me to the bathroom, treats a stray like royalty, and leaves water for me in case I'm thirsty. What a mean man."

Timber hopped onto the passenger seat and leaned over to get a drink of water from the mug Tom had left.

"Don't drink that, Timber. Tom poured something brown from that cup. He's probably poisoning us."

Timber sniffed inside the cup. "You're right. It has a funny smell."

"See."

"It smells like," Timber inhaled, "coffee. But I'll drink it first to make sure the coffee smell isn't poisonous."

Dusti scowled as Timber planted her face into the cup. She put too much trust in bad people and then made him feel stupid for protecting her.

"You win, Dusti," Timber said, backing away from the mug. She batted its handle. "I can't get a drink. The water's down too low."

"You can get anything you want, if you keep trying."

"Sorry, Dust, no matter how hard I try, I can't make my

tongue grow another inch. But if you think you can, be my guest."

Dusti crept between the seats. He peered out the windows and hopped next to Timber. "Sometimes you have to use other means."

Dusti cupped his paw and dipped it inside the cup. A pool of water gathered in his paw. He brought it out, sniffed it, and drank the refreshing water.

"That's neat," Timber said cupping her own paw and thrusting it inside the cup.

"A rule of tongue— if it doesn't work use a paw." Dusti ducked his paw in the mug again and again, lapping up the water as fast as he could.

"I'm glad Tom's winning you over," Timber said. "Trusting someone isn't so bad, is it?"

Dusti snatched his paw out of the mug and marched into the sleeper section. Burrowing under the bed, he glared at Timber. How could she so easily trust Tom and not him? He had been honest with her from the beginning, but she treated him like a liar.

CHAPTER NINE
AGONY

The savory smell of tuna wafted from the passenger seat. Brown circles of cat food spilled from a paper bowl in front of Timber.

Timber held her head away from the bowl as the semi rolled back down the road. Pinching her mouth shut, she furled it around her nose as if the smell was making her sick.

Dusti drooled almost tasting the pungent cat food. He licked his mouth as Timber glanced into the sleeper section. She smiled, buried her head in the bowl, and emphatically crunched the savory morsels.

Each crunch rang with betrayal, stabbing Dusti deeper with every remorseless bite.

Timber lifted her head. A circle of cat food hung around her lower tooth. Her tongue swiped at it as if she purposely stuck it there so Dusti would have to watch her slowly lick it off.

Hollowness ate Dusti. His heart ached.

Grabbing the gold box, he hopped silently back up on the bed. He looked out the window, searching for the letters. The sooner he found them, the sooner they could get away from Tom.

Vehicles of every shape, size, and color flooded the road. Some went at a turtle's pace while others darted in and out of traffic, taking whatever chance they could.

Roads on top of roads stretched out like octopus tentacles. The exits swirled, making it hard to tell which way they were going.

Buildings crowded the roadsides forming towns and cities amidst the clutter.

The sun shined directly above the semi. The Rocky Mountains peaked across the horizon to the west out the left sleeper's window.

A low groan whimpered from the front seat as the buildings thinned. Timber's head drooped as far away from the cat food as it could get.

Tom reached over. He petted Timber and swiped the cat food off the seat.

"ROWW," Timber pleaded.

The semi jerked back as Tom shifted into a higher gear.

A squawk like a chicken blared out of the CB followed by a person's voice.

Tom held five fingers in Timber's face. His voice rose as if begging Timber to do something, but then turned soft as he tucked his thumb into his palm and held up four fingers.

"REOW," Timber said again. She pinned her ears to her

head. She closed her eyes.

Rancid half digested kitty food erupted from Timber's mouth.

Dusti buried his nose under his paws.

Tom's nostrils flared. He glanced at the pile of vomit on the polyester seat.

His rough chapped hands flew towards Timber.

Dusti flinched.

"Timber," Tom said soothingly. His hands slid down Timber's back. He whispered in a gentle voice as he slowed down and took the next exit.

A barrage of semis gathered around a weigh station. A yellow brick office stood next to two standing steel poles.

Tom pulled over before he got to the office. He opened the windows, cleaned up Timber's mess and cat food, and then took her outside into the fresh open air.

Dusti gazed at the open window, longing to go outside, stretch his legs, roll in the dirt, and get some fresh air.

Tom had been very kind and gentle to Timber. Maybe if Dusti told him he was here he'd take him outside, too.

Dusti closed his eyes and covered his ears, ridding his head of Tom's kind actions and Timber's pleas of trust.

Green fields, struggling for life, dotted northern Colorado. Tall cottonwoods cringed in the dry dirt, standing motionless as if the wind no longer existed.

Dusti breathed in deeply, grateful for the steady, unwinding roads. He touched the warm gold box. It felt hotter than human's breath, but as warm as Timber's tongue on his back.

Nothing could live without water, the one commodity that everywhere so desperately needed. Maybe this little box held water from the hot springs near his old home.

Timber yawned and stretched awake as the semi turned right onto a two lane road. Her green eyes glowed like lanterns. Her tail twitched back and forth as if she had never been sick.

Wyoming's empty brown dirt flatlands stretched the minutes into hours. The sound of plucking banjos challenging each other chimed from the stereo speakers, breaking the monotony and bringing solace to Dusti's boredom.

A mild burning sensation tingled in Dusti's bladder as the semi glided into another weigh station. Tom looped the orange twine noose around Timber's neck and took her outside.

Dusti curled his legs under his body and peered out the window.

Wyoming's flat eastern planes spread out like a pancake all around. It didn't look like there'd be letters glowing on a hillside any time soon.

The bed jiggled as the semi chugged back onto the road and then turned onto another small road. The evening sun beat behind the semi as if pushing it onto its destination.

Each agonizing minute danced on Dusti's bladder. Every long hour pounded his kidneys.

Black hills bubbled across the landscape welcoming them to South Dakota. A deep forest perfume slid through the semi's vents. Ponderosa pines shot lengthy, coarse, brown trunks high in the air branching out at the top into a triangular pine needle hood. Arid green and gold grasses stood unmoving under the pines.

A white furry mountain goat stood on the side of the road nibbling the dry grass. His coal black eyes looked directly at Dusti when the semi whisked past him.

Dusti pounded the bed as if trying to slam on the brakes. This was where he needed to be. What if the letters glowed on a hillside just behind the trees?

Tapping his front paws, Dusti's mind raced. He was powerless. He couldn't stop the big rig. He was completely dependent on Tom.

Total darkness wrapped around the semi as the sun faded to nothing. Night's sinister shadows hid the hills, until soft yellow town lights haloed around them.

A blaring yellow glow shined into the windshield as Tom pulled off on the side of the road, cracked open both windows, and hopped out of the semi.

Three-dimensional letters stood above a nearby gas station's roof like Christmas lights. The roof peaked through the middle of the word as a hill glowed in the background.

Dusti grabbed the gold box and jumped onto Tom's seat.

CHAPTER TEN
LETTERS

Dusti stood on his hind legs. He pinned his ears against his head, stretching his front paws through the skinny opening in the window. He slid the box and his mouth across his paws.

His ears sprang up as his head cleared the window.

The window's ridge cut across his front legs. He squirmed, trying to boost his body out, but the window's thin opening held him in a chokehold.

Blood pooled in his face and paws. The air thinned. Darkness closed in on him.

Panicking, Dusti thrashed his head back and forth.

The Pigsie Fairies' box tumbled out of his mouth. It dropped onto the steel step and bounced onto the paved ground.

"RRROOW," he hollered jerking his head back into the semi.

"What happened?" Timber asked.

"I dropped the box."

"You should have waited for Tom," Timber said. "Now the box will be left and we aren't even in the right place."

"We're in the right place," Dusti said.

"Tippy said the Pigsie Fairies are where mountain goats and pronghorns roam. We've seen one mountain goat. You just want out of here so bad, you don't care if you're in the right place or not."

"Tippy also said get out when letters glow on a hillside," Dusti said.

"I haven't seen any—"

Dusti pointed to the letters.

Timber gasped. She pawed at the window. "How do we get out of here?"

Dusti slipped underneath the steering wheel by the driving pedals. "I'm hopping out as soon as Tom opens the door. I'll grab the box and run for the hills."

Dusti studied the driver's door waiting for a crack of open air to peek through.

Loud boots clomped outside the semi. The passenger's door clicked open. Tom held the noose out for Timber. His body blocked the doorway.

Timber ducked into the noose and cuddled in Tom's arms.

Tom grabbed the door to close it.

"MOW," Dusti hollered. He sprang onto the passenger's seat. He belted for the open door, but Tom slammed it shut.

"Great! Tell Tom you're here and he'll take you outside," Dusti said mimicking Timber. "Tom's outside and

I'm still in here."

The door clicked open again. A smile lit up Tom's face as he looped another orange twine noose between his outstretched fingers. "Here, kitty, kitty."

Tom's broad body blocked any escape from the semi. Dusti crept towards the noose as if signing his own death sentence.

Tom glanced at Dusti's twisted tail and then at the driver's side visor. "Dusti?" he asked.

Dusti dropped his tail and slid into the noose.

Tom's calloused hands picked Dusti up like a baby. He cuddled him in one arm, Timber in the other and carried them across the highway into the woods. He tied Dusti's twine to a spruce tree as if giving him privacy to do his business.

Dusti watched as Tom relaxed on the ground and stared at the stars while Timber ran around him. He waved his fingers back and forth coaxing Timber to catch them. A great billowing laugh floated from his mouth as Timber pounced on his whole hand.

Dusti slid his paw between his neck and twine. He pulled the noose loose and wiggled out of it.

"Meow," Dusti whispered in Timber's direction.

Timber squinted Dusti's way.

"Come here," Dusti said waving his paw.

Dusti handed Timber his noose as she ducked under the tree.

"Wha—" Timber asked.

"Stay under the tree and hold my noose while I get the

Pigsie Fairies' box."

"I can't just stay here," Timber said. "We're in this to-geth—"

"I know. I know. I'll come back for you."

Dusti darted from tree to tree, trying not to be seen.

The ground rattled and the air shook as a big diesel truck revved into the nearby gas station.

Dusti squinted toward Tom's semi. It looked like the box was still there.

Hard, thumping music pounded from speakers in the back of a truck. A towhead boy screeched his truck down the road, speeding away without a care in the world.

Dusti's heart beat fast. He ambled over to the semi, staying in the shadows.

The square box sat perfectly upside down by the semi. The far top left corner was dented, but it didn't look like anything else had happened to it.

Dusti grabbed the box's twine in his mouth.

He shuddered as something warm rubbed his back.

"Sorry, I forgot no touching," Timber said. So is it okay?"

"TIMBER." Dusti dropped the box. "Can't you listen? You shouldn't have dropped the twine. Now Tom will be down here, grab both of us, and take us away, messing up everything."

"You of little faith. Of course I didn't drop the twine. I'm not that dumb. And I'm not dumb enough to stay up there and wait for you to conveniently forget about me either."

"I wouldn't leave you. Why can you trust Tom, but you can't trust me?"

"Leaving me in a cornfield and pushing me out of a semi doesn't encourage trust."

"I was protecting you."

"No you weren't. You were protecting yourself."

Timber dodged around Dusti and grabbed the box in her mouth. "Where do we go?"

"Up through the forest to the letters."

"Okay, but first we have to go back to Tom."

"Why?"

"Because it's the right thing to do."

Timber marched into the woods. She spit the box out of her mouth and held her paw on it. "We need to get one thing straight before we go any farther. Without Tom you would have never gotten here. Without him you'd still be stuck in the semi. I understand you don't like Tom, but you still—"

"You don't understand anything. You weren't there when he made Patricia cry. You could never understand how much he hurt her. Sure Tom helped Burt up the stairs, but only after Burt had hit Patricia."

"You're right, Dusti, I didn't see or hear any of that. But I do know how nice Tom has been so far. Did you ever think that maybe he was helping Patricia?"

"By yelling?"

"Maybe he yelled because he was so angry she would let Burt slap her around. Maybe Tom thought the only way she would listen to him and get rid of Burt was by yelling.

Maybe everything he yelled, Patricia wanted to do, but she didn't think she could and that's why she cried. Maybe his yelling helped her."

"Maybe. Maybe you're right."

"Tom and I are connected, Dusti. He knows my name. That's a big thing. I can't leave him without at least telling him thank you. You don't have to, Dusti, but I am." Timber reached down and grabbed the box in her mouth.

Dusti followed Timber under the spruce where he had left her with the twine. The two twine nooses looped around the lowest branch of the spruce.

"Wow, Timber," Dusti said. "That's smart."

Timber shrugged. She sat the box on the ground and yanked both nooses off the tree. She held them in her mouth and trotted toward Tom.

"Meow," Timber said. She bounded into Tom's lap and dropped the nooses. She stood on her back legs, kneaded her front paws on his chest, and gave his cheek a noodgie.

Tom petted Timber. "Good kitty, kitty. Timber, good kitty." He held the twine noose between his fingers, offering it to Timber.

Timber shook her head. She noodgied his cheek again and backed away.

Dusti breathed in the tranquil pine air. He sauntered over to Tom and gave his hand a quick noodgie.

"Dusti," Tom said picking him up. He rubbed Dusti's back. A tear dripped from his eye and landed on Dusti's nose.

Tom's warm hands felt safe around Dusti like he was

where he was supposed to be.

Dusti rubbed the side of his mouth across Tom's hand. He reached up and gave Tom's nose a nice wet noodgie and then dashed under the tree after Timber.

Timber smiled as she held the box in her mouth. "Where do we go now?"

"Up to the letters, I guess."

"Lead the way, Dusti. I'll follow."

CHAPTER ELEVEN
BILLIE

Huge gray boulders stood like sentinels underneath the large glowing letters. Their porous surface fell down in sheets, making it impossible to climb.

Dusti and Timber scurried around the front of the boulders. They climbed up a hill to the left, crept through an army of ponderosa pines, and looped around to the back of the boulders. The boulders rough jagged backside ascended to the letters, making crooked mismatched steps.

Dusti jumped onto the first boulder lip, and then onto the next and the next with Timber following close behind him. He crouched down on the thin boulder's edge before the top and studied his last jump. It stretched higher than Dusti had ever jumped before without a running start.

"Can you make that jump?" Timber asked.

Dusti crouched low and jumped as high as he could. He reached for the top of the boulder, grasping onto its lip. He curled his clawless paws around its edge and hung there.

His paws slipped.

Timber's paws shoved against Dusti's haunches, launching him in the air. His pads tingled and cracked as he landed four-footed on top of the boulder.

"You didn't have to do that," Dusti said as Timber bounded up next to him.

"I know. I could have let you fall, but I thought what the heck."

Dusti stalked around a boulder to the front of the letters.

A dull yellow light glowed from the letters metal frames and shined down on a small town.

Two black eyes stared from behind the last tan metal letter frame.

Dusti squirmed back to the first letter. He held out his forepaw ready to attack.

A knocking rang from the boulders as the pursuer crept closer. A white beard ruffled from his long chin. Two black pointy horns glared in the letter's light.

Timber dropped the box by Dusti's paws. "Hi, Mr. Mountain Goat."

"Are you insane?" Dusti asked. "You can't talk to him. He's a goat. You're a cat."

"Maybe he can help us," Timber said.

"Or spear us with his two pointy horns."

A deep bleating laugh floated over the hills. "I'm not gonna eat ya, Dusti."

Dusti's fur on his spine flared.

"Don't act so surprised," the mountain goat said. "All living creatures could understand each other if they only listened a bit closer. I'm here to help. Name is Billie. I have to get ya to the Pigsie Fairies as the sun starts to rise. I wasn't expecting two of ya, but a spunky friend always makes journeys more worthwhile."

"I'm not his friend yet," Timber said. "But will be someday. My name's Timber."

Dusti grabbed the gold box and darted over to the last letter. "Where do we go?"

"Hold on there, kitty," Billie said, kneeling down. "Ya need to hop on my back."

"I'd rather walk," Dusti said as Timber hopped on Billie's back.

"Suit yourself," Billie said. "I didn't know kitty paws could handle such rough terrain. My hooves have wonderful traction for rocky, rugged ground. I hope you can keep up."

Dusti's pads tingled already from the short climb. He glared at his tender paws, clamped the box in his mouth, and hopped onto Billie's back behind Timber.

Dusti curled his paws, clinging onto Billie's coarse white hair. His body swayed as Billie stood up. He tried to stay balanced on Billie's thin spine, but couldn't grasp onto anything with his clawless forepaws.

Dusti sighed. He looked at Timber's front legs wrapped around Billie's neck.

"Wait, Billie," Dusti said. "Timber and I need to switch places. I can't hold on back here. I don't have any front claws."

"It takes a strong kid, goat or cat, to admit their problems," Billie said kneeling down. "But every problem or set back is just another obstacle waiting to be overcome."

Dusti hugged his front legs around Billie's neck.

Timber wrapped her front legs around Dusti and snuggled her head on Dusti's back.

Dusti squirmed under Timber's tight hold. "How far away are the Pigsie Fairies?"

"About fifteen miles," Billie said. "A lot farther than I can walk before sunrise."

Dusti tensed his back claws digging them into Billie's back.

"Hold on there, kitty," Billie said. "Clawing my back won't get ya there any faster. I'm only taking ya a mile or two. Then two mule deer, Buck and Junior, will carry ya. They'll go a lot faster than me. We'll get ya to the Pigsie Fairies as the sun rises, I promise."

Stars twinkled over the tall green ponderosa pines. The cool, stale air hung in the sky as if the warmth from the day had carried into the night. The smell of pine cloaked the trees, not venturing far from its source.

An eerie stillness wrapped around the hills. The stark quietness emphasized the rattle of each pine needle and snap of every twig.

Dusti buried his head into Billie's white soft hump of fur that surrounded his neck. His eyes grew heavy. The rhythmic clotting of Billie's hooves made a soft melody echoing through the forest.

Sliding his protruding bottom canine tooth between the box and twine, Dusti secured the box in case he fell asleep.

*   *   *

An exploding snort woke Dusti. He gripped Billie around the neck and dug his back claws into Billie's back as they jolted downhill into a gully.

Billie bleated. "Buck, it's Billie. Dusti brought a spunky cat with him. I hope Junior doesn't mind carrying her."

Two massive, reddish brown deer clambered through the gully. Their black nostrils fluttered as they snorted. The larger deer's antlers looked like an upside down chandelier, branching out into five main points. The smaller deer's antlers only forked.

"Junior's never carried anything before," Buck said. "If you can carry both of them, I know I can."

"Don't get your antlers in a wad, Buck," Billie said, kneeling down and letting Timber and Dusti jump off his back. "I only had to carry them for a mile and a half. You and Junior have a lot farther to go. I'm sure Junior will be fine."

Junior trotted over to Timber. "I'll give you the safest ride you've ever had; it'll feel like you're floating. It'll be better than ol' muley could do on his best day."

"Be careful, Junior," Buck said. "Some ol' muleys might take that as a challenge." He winked, dropped his chin, protruded his antlers, and stalked toward Junior.

"I was only joking," Junior said. "I know you'll at least keep up with me."

Buck and Junior knelt down before Dusti and Timber. Dusti climbed onto Buck's coarse back as Timber climbed onto Junior's.

Dusti gripped his forepaws tightly around Buck's neck as Billie bleated good-bye.

Buck's long legs trotted fast across the uneven ground. They landed directly underneath his body as if he were walking in place. His sharp shoulder blade chafed Dusti's stomach.

Junior raced ahead. His ribs poked out of his side.

"The earth is changing," Buck said. "Much of our food has been taken. A great fiery inferno raged across eighty-four thousand acres of our hills taking our food, air, and even some of our lives.

"After this happened the temperature and weather did not change, but stayed in limbo. No wind, no temperature change, no weather patterns, no rain."

Buck dropped his antlers. "No rain, no food. Whatever's in that little box will save what has already been destroyed."

A dusty smell of ash overcast the airy scent of pine. Naked, charred tree trunks shadowed the forest as Buck and Junior trotted for miles.

The dark morning sky clung to the lifeless hills.

Buck and Junior climbed up a steep rocky incline. Pine trees and grasses covered the rocky hill as if somehow it had been protected from the fiery inferno.

Hiding in the deep grass, Buck and Junior bedded down, curling their legs under them.

"What're you doing?" Dusti asked.

"This is far as we go," Buck said. "It's almost dawn. It's time for deer to bed down."

Dusti paced over to the hill's ridge. He could never make it down before sunrise.

Buck smiled and yawned. "Don't worry, Dusti. The Pigsie Fairies will find you. You and Timber should nap, too. I'm sure you have a long day ahead of you."

Timber curled between Junior's legs. Soon soft snores bleated from Junior and Buck and a humming purr rumbled from Timber.

Dusti's heart pounded against his chest. He stalked from tree to tree trying to calm his nerves, but adrenaline poured through his body. It would be better if he didn't have to depend on others. Then he could get to where he needed to be so much faster.

Dusti dropped to the ground and hung his paws over the hill's ridge. He shook his head. Without Tom, Billie, Buck, and Timber's help he wouldn't have gotten here or gotten here nearly this fast. He knew he would always have to depend on others.

Dusti looked at his clawless forepaws. He only wished others could depend on him.

CHAPTER TWELVE
THE CAVE

An iridescent pink glow rested over the hills as the sun rose. Charred land and trees stretched over acres and acres. Fire had licked the green and gold grasses into a deep auburn. Piles of trees lay on the ground as if the hills had become a mass grave instead of a source of life.

Dusti clasped the Pigsie Fairies' box in his mouth. The drought had destroyed this section of the United States. How much longer until it destroyed the rest?

Timber sat by Dusti, stretching awake. "What are you thinking about?"

Dusti pointed towards the burned hills. "We're too late. How can this little box repair all of this destruction?"

A giggle twittered out of a pine tree. A fairy the size of a humming bird flew down from the top branches like an angel. Two blonde curlicued pigtails sat on both sides of her baby shaped face. Deep dimples dug into her cheeks as she smiled.

"You silly, you aren't late," the Pigsie Fairy said.

"You're just in time."

Dusti nudged the box toward the Pigsie Fairy, "Here, this is for you."

"It's not for me. You have to give it to Queen Pigsie."

Dusti squinted at the tree the Pigsie Fairy had come out of.

"She's not in there. She's at the Palace in the Pigsie Fairy Cave." The Pigsie Fairy shook her head as tears trickled out of her brown, almond shaped eyes. "Our cave used to breathe, but ever since the weather stopped changing, it doesn't anymore."

"Where is the Pigsie Fairy Cave," Timber asked.

"Just a little way farther," the Pigsie Fairy said, "about five miles. We have to get to the cave before the sun completely rises."

"Timber and I can't walk that far," Dusti said. He nudged the box closer to the Pigsie Fairy. "Please, just give this to her."

"No, Dusti, you have to give it to her yourself," the Pigsie Fairy said.

She flew around, over, and under Timber. "I didn't know there would be two of you. Timber does make things difficult. She's skinny, though. She should be easy enough to carry."

"Little you can't carry Timber and me," Dusti said.

"No, silly, I couldn't even carry one fat cat, let alone two." The Pigsie Fairy curled her lips around her sparkling white teeth. A sharp, loud whistle rang from her lips.

Fifty baby-faced Pigsie Fairies with the same brown,

almond shaped eyes zoomed out of the trees like a swarm of bees. Their blonde curlicued pigtails swung in the breeze from their transparent wings.

"We have two cats to transport today," the Pigsie Fairy said. She pointed at thirty fairies, "You will carry Dusti. And you others will carry Timber. She looks lighter, so there doesn't need to be as many of you carrying her. I'll lead the way."

Dusti gripped the box in his mouth as an assortment of fairies floated above him. Two lines of fairies grabbed either of his sides and then another line grabbed above his spine away from his cut. Their tiny fingers pinched his skin.

Within seconds Dusti and Timber were airborne, miles in the air. The hilly ground below looked like a lumpy patchwork quilt, filled with greens, browns, circles, and rectangles.

Dusti gulped down his queasy stomach, grateful he didn't have anything in it. He closed his eyes happy he was born a cat and not a bird.

The lead Pigsie Fairy flew backwards, shouting orders at her crews. Her voice, though sharp and clear, joined with the humming wings as if she was singing along to a song they were playing.

"Veer right," the lead Pigsie Fairy said.

Dusti's body wrenched to the side as every Pigsie Fairy made a hairpin turn to the right.

"We're almost home," the lead Pigsie Fairy said. "Descend softly. Remember you're carrying precious cargo."

Gold grasses waved under Dusti's paws as the Pigsie Fairies descended toward a gray boulder swelling out of the ground. A stone corral circled around the boulder.

The lead Pigsie Fairy buzzed over the corral. "Cats, tuck in your legs."

Dusti curled his back legs to his stomach and folded his forelegs across his chest. The Pigsie Fairies flew over the corral and darted toward a small oval hole in the bottom of the boulder.

"Squeeze together, girls," the lead Pigsie Fairy said zooming through the hole.

Dusti's Pigsie Fairies lay across his back and squeezed his sides as they went through the oval opening. A hollow echoing sound trembled from their wings into the stark obscurity below. A cool dampness clung to the cave.

The Pigsie Fairies descended through a maze of passages as if they could see in the dark.

Dusti tried to control his stomach as air whizzed past his face. He hoped the Pigsie Fairies knew where they were going and the cave wouldn't close up on him.

His stomach rubbed on the gritty stone floor. He reached down trying to grasp onto something that would lift him up.

A viridian aura of light shone down a passage to the right. Dusti blinked his eyes thinking they were playing tricks on him, but when he opened them the light shined brighter.

"Cats, drop your paws," the lead Pigsie Fairy said. "You can walk now."

The sharp stone floor dug into Dusti's paws as the Pigsie Fairies released him. He waited for Timber to catch up and then followed the Pigsie Fairies towards the light.

Magnificent features extended across the cave walls and ceilings. White, shimmering crystals dotted the walls as if they were petrified snowflakes and icicles. Thin lines of brown calcite crisscrossed over the ceiling in a honeycomb formation.

The lead Pigsie Fairy stopped in a circular section of the passage where the light was brightest. "Welcome to the Palace," she said.

She nodded at the other Pigsie Fairies. "Good job, teams. Please sit down. It's time to rest."

Leaving them, she flew into a small crevice in the honeycombed wall.

Dusti sat on his hind legs and set the gold box on the floor. The cluster of Pigsie Fairies that had carried him leaned against his sides. Their thin wings drooped, slowly fluttering up and down as if gasping for breath.

Stalactites dropped from the top of the cave as stalagmites grew from the floor. Water ran slowly down a brown stone making it look like peanut butter. Small drips of calcite clung to the wet stone's surface. Soft iridescent lights gleamed from clusters of upside down mushroom mounds on the ceiling.

"How do you make those lights," Dusti asked.

"Through bioluminescence," a Pigsie Fairy said. She lay on Timber's back, crossed her hands behind her head, and stared up at the ceiling. "Our cousins, the

Lightning Pixies, can make yellow light with their body. Since we can't do that, they taught us how to use certain fungi for the same results, so we aren't living in the dark."

Dusti gazed at the mushroom lights mesmerized by their enchanting glow.

A soft tinkle hummed through the cave as the lead Pigsie Fairy floated out of the crevice. She glided in front of Dusti and loudly cleared her throat, "HUMPH, HUMPH, I present to you Queen Pigsie."

An old, wrinkled Pigsie Fairy flew out of the crevice holding a twisted wooden cane. Her gray curlicued pig-tailed hair bounced as she descended toward Dusti and landed in front of him.

Her tiny, withered hand patted Dusti's forepaw as she leaned on her cane.

"You have traveled a great distance," Queen Pigsie began. "I never thought I would be the queen who would see you, Dusti. I am honored, but at the same time disappointed. You come because there has been much destruction."

"The earth is changing," Queen Pigsie said in her weathered, childlike voice, "not only big grand changes, but also small changes that are only noticed by those affected by it. Here in our cave we have been affected by one of these small changes. Our cave used to breathe, but ever since the fiery inferno it hasn't."

Dusti set the box on the ground and nudged it toward Queen Pigsie. "I don't know if this will directly help you, but I'm sure it will somehow."

"Do you know what's in the box?" Queen Pigsie asked.

"No," Dusti said, "but it has to be water. That's the only thing that makes sense."

"Some things don't make sense in the present, but they do in the past."

"I don't understand."

"Someday in the future you will, someday."

Queen Pigsie sat on the box and grabbed the orange twine. It was like a big rope in her tiny hands. She struggled to untie it, looping her small fingers between the knots.

Silence enfolded the cave, disturbed only by the steady drip of water off the stalactites.

The Pigsie Fairies stood rigid as if holding their breath in anticipation.

Timber's eyes followed each movement Queen Pigsie's hands made.

Dusti held his breath trying to quiet the loud pounding of his heart.

Queen Pigsie bundled the twine around her hands and crawled off the lid. "Dusti, will you do the honors?"

Dusti twitched his whiskers. He stood up and held his head high trying to hide his quivering paws and shaking body.

Queen Pigsie grabbed his paw and placed it on top of the box. "Feel this. What does it feel like? What does it remind you of?"

"It's warm like kitty's breath," Dusti said. He stared at the ground and whispered, "It reminds me of Timber cleaning my back."

"Open it," Queen Pigsie said.

Dusti nudged the lid off with his nose. He glanced in-side.

It was empty.

CHAPTER THIRTEEN
SACRIFICE

Dusti exhaled loudly.

A hot gust of wind exploded from the box. It wrapped around Dusti, sucking his breath away.

The wind rushed from the Palace. It burst through the cave. A faint whistle bounded through the passages. It echoed like the semi had when it drove through the tunnels.

Dusti tried to inhale, but the wind was like a vacuum connected to his mouth, sucking out all of his air. No matter what he did or how much air he needed, he could not breathe.

A loud screech like a teakettle reverberated from the cave's opening.

Dusti crumpled on the ground, fighting for breath.

"He made our cave breathe, again!" the Pigsie Fairies shouted. "He made our cave breathe again!" They grabbed each other's hands, circled around Dusti, danced, sang, and cried.

Cold oxygen filtered through Dusti's nostrils and into

his lungs, but, however hard he breathed, he could not get enough air into his lungs or through his body.

"Dusti," a Pigsie Fairy said clutching his paw, "don't you understand? Because of you our cave can breathe."

"I don't," Dusti gasped, "understand . . . how this . . . will help."

Timber lay next to Dusti as Queen Pigsie patted his head.

"It will help," Queen Pigsie said. Strength beamed out of her hand. "Give it time and it will. Rest. It is time to sleep."

Dusti couldn't sleep. If he closed his eyes, he feared, he might never wake up again. There was so much he still had to do. He couldn't leave the world without finding Ryan. Ryan needed to know how much he loved him. He could not leave the world without giving Ryan a proper good-bye.

Dusti panted as images of the last good-bye he had had with Ryan raced through his mind.

Ryan slung a yellow backpack over his shoulder. He picked up Dusti and carried him through the huge empty house. The assaulting, acrid smell of bleach radiated from the walls and floors.

Ryan crept up the stairs. He slid across the ceramic tile landing and quietly pulled open the front door as if he was running away.

The first rays of morning light sparkled on the loaded moving van in the driveway. Ryan carried Dusti into the nearby forest. He dug in his pocket and pulled out two medicine bottles.

After Dusti's jaw broke, Burt had brought medicine home from the veterinary clinic where he worked. Even though the medicine relieved the throbbing in Dusti's lower jaw, it couldn't straighten his jaw back to the way it was. His lower jaw now sat to the left of his top jaw causing his left, bottom canine tooth to rest against the outside of his upper lip.

Ryan set Dusti on the pine needle covered ground. His knees dug into Dusti's shoulders as he held him firmly between his legs.

Dusti growled as Ryan wrenched the liquid medicine and a dry pill into his mouth.

Dusti gagged.

Ryan held Dusti's mouth shut until the hard pill finally dropped down his throat.

Dusti cuddled in Ryan's arms inhaling his warm cinnamon scent as they crossed a vacant highway and slunk down a long dirt driveway.

The smell of diesel, salt, and sulfur beaded the valley air. A pea green house with a gabled roof sat on one side of the driveway while a maroon semi parked on the other side.

Ryan snuck up the three whitewashed steps to the front porch. He pulled a sheet of folded yellow paper and the medicine out of his pockets and then yanked a bag of cat food and a dish out of the backpack. Unfolding the yellow paper, he laid it on the wooden porch with the two bottles of medicine on top and the cat food and dish to the side.

Ryan hugged Dusti and stroked his back. He kissed Dusti's head in between his ears.

Dusti noodgied Ryan's freckled nose.

Ryan rubbed away tears with the back of his hand. He set Dusti on the porch next to the cat food, medicine, and yellow paper. He whispered human words Dusti didn't understand.

Dusti rubbed his scent glands on Ryan's palm and on his jeans. He purred and then noodgied Ryan's hand.

Ryan reached down as if he would stroke Dusti's back, but unclipped his collar instead. He fisted his hand around the collar, glared in the direction of his house, and jammed his fisted hand in his pocket. He hopped off the steps and kicked his way down the driveway stirring up huge clouds of dust.

Dusti hopped off the porch. This wasn't right. They were supposed to run away together. "Mow," he called running down the driveway.

Ryan yelled. He pointed at the porch and ran away.

Dusti sat in the dirt driveway. How could Ryan leave him at a stranger's house? Did he not need him anymore? Was it because he hadn't protected Patricia?

Dusti shook his head. He scrambled down the driveway and ran to Ryan's house.

By the time Dusti got to Ryan's house, the moving van was rolling down the street. Patricia's car backed out of the driveway.

Ryan sat in the backseat of Patricia's car. Tears streamed down his face. His body swayed as if he was crying on the inside, too.

As the car turned onto the following street, Dusti glimpsed a silver heart gleaming on Ryan's upper arm.

Dusti knew that heart. It had his name etched in it.

The heart had dangled from the collar he had worn around his neck. Now it dangled from the collar Ryan wore around his arm.

Dusti's body shook as cold, lonely tears puddled on the stone ground.

Timber put a reassuring paw on Dusti's back.

He would not let himself die. He would not let one more thing ruin his chance of being with Ryan. The cave could have the breath it had taken from him, but that was all it was getting. Dusti would never quit until he knew Ryan was okay.

He shut his eyes. He was tired. It was time to sleep.

CHAPTER FOURTEEN
THE MEAL

The moist aroma of trout slithered up Dusti's nostrils, waking him from a sound sleep. Gasping for breath, Dusti stretched awake to the gentle hum of Pigsie Fairy wings and the echo of the cave's whistle.

The Pigsie Fairies zoomed around the cave carrying stones and pebbles past a thick stalagmite. Timber snored next to Dusti, still lost in deep sleep.

Dusti huffed for breath as he very slowly stood up.

Timber's eyes shot open. She jumped up next to Dusti. "How are you feeling?"

"Better. I can't . . . breathe well," Dusti said. He huffed for breath. "Air has been . . . twisted from . . . my lungs. I can't catch . . . my breath."

Timber sniffed and blinked her eyes. She patted Dusti's paw and cleared her throat. "This is just a set back. You're a strong cat. You can overcome anything."

"Yes, you can," Queen Pigsie said floating over to them. "But let's not think of set backs now. After nineteen hours of sleep, I'm sure you two are starving. It's time to fill our tummies with a breakfast in our guests honor. Follow me."

Dusti huffed behind Timber as she followed Queen Pigsie around the stalagmite.

Eighty Pigsie Fairies stood in a circle. Small pebble cups and stone plates adorned with chunks of trout decorated the ground in front of them.

A sunrise pink glowed on the Pigsie Fairies' cheeks as if the cave's breath had kissed merriment into them. Their almond brown eyes sparkled. Their iridescent wings fluttered with a new awakened hope.

Queen Pigsie led Timber and Dusti to the head of the circle where two full-size, fresh caught trout as long as Dusti sat on either side of Queen Pigsie's miniscule plate. Crystal mountain water glittered from large oval stone bowls above the trout.

Dusti collapsed next to his food. He tried to slow his breathing, grasping onto any air he could get into his lungs.

Queen Pigsie squatted down, grabbed her pebble cup and raised it in front of her. "I'd like to purpose two toasts before we eat."

The Pigsie Fairies squatted and picked up their cups.

Queen Pigsie turned toward Dusti. "It took a great deal of courage and strength to come all this way with someone you *thought* had wronged your family. It takes even greater strength to hold onto life especially when everything is trying to destroy it. Our cave breathes again because of you, but more importantly so do you."

"Here, here," the Pigsie Fairies said clinking their stone

cups against each other's cups.

A fairy raised her cup toward Timber.

"Sorry, no opposable thumbs," Timber said holding out a paw.

"That's okay," the fairy said and clinked her cup on Timber's bowl.

"Our next toast goes to Timber," Queen Pigsie said turning to her. "You are a true and loyal friend. It's hard suffering through your own struggles, but even harder when someone you love suffers and you can't do anything about it. You sat by Dusti after the wind had taken his breath. You would not sleep until Dusti's breathing was more rhythmic. Anyone, animal, fairy, or person, would be lucky to have you as a friend."

Dusti's head spun. Timber had done so much for him and all she wanted in return was a friend. Instead he had returned her kindness, her friendship, with degradation, meanness, and loathing.

Queen Pigsie loudly cleared her throat and raised her cup one more time. "I wish even greater success on journeys and tasks yet to come."

The Pigsie Fairies tapped their cups politely while staring at their food.

A merry laugh tinkled from Queen Pigsie. "Okay, I understand. Let's not waste any more time talking while there's delicious fish in front of us. Dig in."

All of the Pigsie Fairies crossed their legs and sat down in a flourish. They ripped off slivers of trout with their small fingers and ate the trout as if it was finger food.

Dusti nibbled the trout, gasping between every bite. The oily flavors of fresh, raw fish burst against his taste buds. A pure tang of cool undiluted mountain water hung on every bite calming the fish's sharp oily taste.

Wheezing, Dusti picked the last piece of meat off the bone. He lapped the icy mountain water from his bowl.

As the feast concluded Queen Pigsie stood once again. "Friends, now that our tummies are full and our bodies are hydrated, it is time I present Dusti with his next task."

Dusti's ears perked up. He looked around the cave.

The Pigsie Fairies smiled and breathed in the fresh wind blowing through their cave.

Timber's mouth gaped open. "What? Another task? How many more tasks does Dusti have to do?"

"I only ask one of him," Queen Pigsie said.

"Dusti can't do another task," Timber said. "He can't breathe. He barely walks two feet and practically passes out. How dare you expect another task from him when you're the one that took his breath."

"You have every right to be angry, Timber," Queen Pigsie said. "When someone we love suffers from means beyond our control it's normal to lash out. I would never ask more of Dusti than what he can handle."

"What will he lose with this next task, his hearing, his sight? No, Dusti's not going."

"The United States is still imbalanced, Timber. Disasters will continue seizing life across the land until the elements are balanced or the United States is ruined."

"Then send me instead."

"No," Dusti said.

Timber opened her mouth, but Dusti cut her off.

"Timber, hush," Dusti said. "I can fight . . . my own battles."

Timber smirked at Queen Pigsie.

"What's the next task?" Dusti asked.

"You're not thinking Dust," Timber said. "Not enough oxygen is getting to your brain. You're not going. I am."

"You just want . . . all the glory," Dusti said, batting at Timber's whiskers.

Timber pinned her whiskers across the side of her face.

Dusti sucked in a mouthful of air. "Timber . . . I have to do this . . . for you . . . for Ryan, for everyone . . . but I can't do it . . . without you."

"You can't do it at all," Timber said. "I'm going, not you."

"Unfortunately, Timber," Queen Pigsie said, "Dusti has to do this task. We cannot send you in his place."

A loud whistle from the wind echoed throughout the cave.

The Pigsie Fairies grabbed each other in hugs. Their dimples dug deeper into their cheeks as they smiled.

"Look how happy . . . we made them," Dusti said. "Won't you help me . . . one more time?"

Timber heaved a big sigh. "Where else would I go?"

CHAPTER FIFTEEN
CAPRIHORN, TILO, AND PRONG

The drone of Pigsie Fairy wings echoed throughout the cave as they floated above Dusti and Timber.

Queen Pigsie tied a thin string resembling fishing twine around Dusti's neck. A cylindrical gray stone vial dangled from the string and ended halfway down Dusti's legs.

Grabbing the vial, Queen Pigsie scooted it around to Dusti's shoulders.

"You and this vial will get on a train," Queen Pigsie said. "Days will pass as you ride across the plains. Sometimes the track junctions into a Y, at these locations you'll need to decide, which track you'll take— North, South, East, or West, the end and beginning aren't always best.

"But when you see where Magnolias grow, remember east is not the way to go. Ride the next train; soon its track will be done. Then ride a short line towards the setting sun. Soon you'll encounter a greater feat, where Pixie Dust covers the cars and streets. Feelings you thought you'd never again know, will find you all around our family's home."

Dusti nodded digesting every word as quickly as it was

spoken.

Queen Pigsie's thin arm reached out. She grabbed Dusti's chin in her tiny hand. "One word of warning before your journey begins— be cautious of winged or fine limbed creatures, not all of them will be your friends."

The Pigsie Fairies' tiny hands wove through Dusti's fur and grabbed his skin. They lifted him in the air, zoomed into the cave passages, and out into the forest.

Thick, gray clouds hid the morning sun. Dark shadows crept along the plains, hills, and into the forest.

Humid wind ruffled the Pigsie Fairies' pigtails as they flew southwest.

Five pronghorns paced impatiently through the burned forest. Their white rump hairs stood rigid as if warning of danger.

"You're late," a pronghorn said glaring at the Pigsie Fairies.

"Don't mind, Caprihorn," another pronghorn said. "He forgets we're the fastest mammals on this hemisphere. Caprihorn and I will carry the cats. My name's Tilo."

The Pigsie Fairies dropped Dusti and Timber on the pronghorns' backs. They looked up at the dark sky and then at the sodden ground. Their wings tinkled like wind chimes in the humid wind. "Thank you, Dusti and Timber. The earth is changing for the better because of you."

Dusti gripped between the two white bands of hair that circled Tilo's neck as the pronghorns dashed away from the Pigsie Fairies. They trotted together in a tight bunch through the wet forest, and then spread out in a single file line.

Timber held a death grip on Caprihorn's neck as he raced in front of Tilo, taking the lead of the small herd. He wove in and out of trees, through the forest, down the hill, and stopped at a barbed wire fence separating the hills from another stretch of prairie.

Tilo bent down on his knees with the other pronghorns. "Get off, Dusti. I can't crawl under the fence with you on my back."

Dusti hopped onto the muddy brown soil. "Why don't you . . . leap over the fence?"

"Don't know," Tilo said. "Never tried." He folded his long legs underneath him, ducked his head, and shimmied under the barbed wire fence.

Dusti walked under the fence, hopped on Tilo's back, and tried to catch his breath.

Wet auburn grasses feathered across the burned prairie clinging to the rain they had gotten the previous night.

Bubbly forest hills sprang up on either side of the plains. Strong ponderosa pines barely licked by the fire guarded the hills.

The sinister smell of tar lashed against the harmony of pine and rain as the pronghorns followed a black paved highway that cut through the forest and stretched across the plains.

The plains swept out like a sheet of paper flattening the hills into the background. A skinny river tickled the prairie shores. Its unmoving glassy surface made a perfect reflection of the foggy indigo sky.

Pronged black horns bounced above the long golden grasses on the other side of the river.

Tilo, Caprihorn, and the other pronghorns stood on the riverbank. They stared at the rippling river as if they didn't know what to do.

"How do we . . . get across?" Dusti asked.

"Swim," Tilo said.

"I don't swim," Dusti said.

"You don't have to swim. Just hang onto my back and I'll get you across. Hold on tight, the water is moving faster since the rain came."

Dusti gripped Tilo's neck.

Freezing droplets of water burst across Dusti's fur as the pronghorns plunged into the river breaking the glassy surface. The sharp water beat furiously against them, pooling around Dusti and washing over Tilo's back.

The pronghorns held their heads high as the strong current pushed them down river.

Tilo reached his forelegs out and crawled in a doggy paddle across, fighting against the river's force. His hind legs sank to the riverbed. Kicking against it, he sprang his body forward.

Dusti clung onto Tilo's tense neck. He wanted to stand on his tippy paws away from the water, but didn't want to lose the traction his paws held on Tilo's back.

A tall, burly pronghorn met them on the other side of the river. Taut muscles gleamed through his reddish brown hair. He stood tall and stout like an army officer. "What's taken so long? The train's almost here."

"Sorry, Prong," Tilo said inching his way up onto the riverbank.

"I have others from my herd waiting on the track," Prong said.

"Good, that should stop the train."

"No, it won't," said Caprihorn, splashing out of the river. "It takes a mile for a train to stop. They can't just slam on the brakes."

"But they'll blow a warning whistle to get the pronghorns off the track," Prong said. "We're about two miles away. Run three-fourths your speed. That should get us there on time. If you hear the whistle, run full force."

Prong raced ahead of Caprihorn, guiding the herd through the prairie.

Timber slid down Caprihorn's back as he ran after Prong. She bit him between the shoulders hanging on for dear life.

Tilo's front legs soared while his hind legs launched him forward. He threw his tongue out to the side. A long trail of saliva smacked Dusti across the face.

Dusti dug his hind claws into Tilo. The vial beat against his back.

Tilo's legs became a blur of motion as he sped forty-five miles an hour across the prairie. A warm breeze whisked past his face. He didn't pant or heave, but opened his mouth and threw out his tongue letting the breeze fill his lungs.

Dusti buried his head into Tilo's stiff neck, dodging the saliva flying from Tilo's mouth.

A succession of short toots whistled through the air. Tilo's neck tightened.

Caprihorn's rump hair shined.

Prong dropped his head below his shoulders and ran.

Caprihorn and Tilo followed at full speed as the other three pronghorns hurtled out of their way. The gold grass whipped across their body. Their legs disappeared as if they were flying through the air.

Dusti's whiskers pelted against his face.

The rhythmic sound of metal wheels rumbled across the plains. A sharp string of whistles blasted in time to the beat of the train.

Two pronghorns dove into the tall grass as a long train with orange emblems stamped across the cars rolled onto the tracks. The locomotive pushed a rectangular black metal plate that looked like a snowplow.

Tilo, Prong, and Caprihorn belted out of the grass. They raced along the plowed dirt by the track. They sped toward an open boxcar near the rear of the train.

The train's cadenced beat vibrated the ground.

"You need to jump," Tilo yelled. He evened out with the boxcar, running along its side.

Dusti hunched up his hind end, but couldn't rip his paws away from Tilo's neck.

Timber leaped through the air. She landed in the box-car. Caprihorn blended into the sidelines.

"I can't keep up with the train," Tilo said. "You need to jump."

Dusti gulped. He wrenched his paws away from Tilo's

neck, closed his eyes, and jumped into the fast moving air.

CHAPTER SIXTEEN
HARD-HEARTED

Dusti's pads tore across a slick metal floor. His hind claws sprang out and screeched across the metal as he cuffed his forepaws, grasping onto the slippery ground.

A tightness wrapped around Dusti's throat cutting off his limited air supply. He coughed. His legs tingled. He crumpled to the ground.

Heavy, gray dust drifted around him as if he was floating in the clouds. The smell of flour and coffee emanated from the plywood sides of the empty boxcar. A steady tremor pounded against his legs. The bounds around his neck grew tighter as if someone was yanking on the vial, stealing what he had to deliver.

Dusti leaped to his paws, knocking off whatever was on his back.

Timber tumbled across the boxcar. Her green eyes glowed in the darkness.

Dusti coughed. The pressure on his neck had lessened as if the vial wasn't there anymore. He gulped the chalky air.

"What were you . . . doing?"

"I was helping you," Timber said.

"By stealing. I thought I could . . . trust you, Timber. I thought you were . . . my friend."

"I didn't steal the vial. I untwisted the string so you could breathe better."

Dusti turned his head and looked at his shoulders. The stone vial sat perfectly between his shoulder blades. The string kinked as if it had been twisted.

"I'm only trying to be your friend," Timber said, "and you treat me like an enemy. Do you have any compassion or are you so hard-hearted from past wrongs that you can't even appreciate someone who is helping you?"

Dusti dropped his head. Timber's words pierced his heart like a dull, rusty knife leaving its poison behind. Regrettably everything she said was true. "I'm sorry, Timber."

"Don't worry, Dusti. This will end the way you want; I'll fade into the background after you save the United States and not even get the respect of a memory."

"Come on, Tim. It won't be . . . that way. I promise."

"Empty promises are worth as much as the thought that goes into them." Timber turned away from Dusti and walked into the shadows of the boxcar.

Dusti brushed his paw across the dusty ground and sat in the doorway, watching the plains roll by. He wasn't giving Timber an empty promise. He could never forget her no matter how hard he tried.

*   *   *

Big strong, hairy bison dotted the grasslands. Sparse cedar trees replaced the bison as the train sped through the plains and onto Nebraska's stark lonely prairie. Wind whipped the cedar trees' thin, needled limbs towards the southeast and threw gusts of sand against the train.

A loud squeal clanged from the right wheels as the train turned right. The wheels on the other side echoed as if they were skipping across the rails like a rock skipping across water.

Two tracks of rail crept closer together. When they crossed a steel X linked them together until they divided back into their two separate tracks.

The train slowed. It rocked heavily back and forth as if it wanted to throw Dusti out into the bare prairie. It jolted as the wheels slid into and then out of the steel X.

Longing for the security the semi had given him, Dusti crept to a far corner of the boxcar. He quieted his labored breathing so he wouldn't wake Timber and thought about Queen Pigsie's riddle.

"You and this vial will get on a train. Days will pass as you ride across the plains. Sometimes the track junctions into a Y, at these locations you'll need to decide, which track you'll take— North, South, East, or West, the end and beginning aren't always best. But when you see where Magnolias grow, remember east is not the way to go. Ride the next train; soon its track will be done. Then ride a short line towards the setting sun."

That was pretty self explanatory. He'd ride south and east across the plains until he got to a short line, whatever that was, and then ride west. But who got the vial, where would he end up? What would he lose with this next task?

Dusti slowly whispered the last four lines of Queen Pigsie's riddle. *"Soon you'll encounter a greater feat, where Pixie Dust covers the cars and streets. Feelings you thought you'd never again know, will find you all around our family's home."*

The last four lines pounded through Dusti's mind, leaving a very real, but unidentifiable, trace. What feat? What feelings? Whose family's home? What was Pixie Dust?

Closing his eyes, he thought of everything the Pigsie Fairies had said to him and what he had seen in their cave.

A blue flash of light skidded through his mind.

The Pigsie Fairies had learned to make light from their cousins— the Lightning Pixies, but their light glowed yellow not blue. Pixie Dust must glow yellow, too.

Dusti rolled his tense shoulders, sliding the vial around his neck.

A very faint rattle shifted through the vial as it changed positions.

Dusti held the vial in his paws. It didn't feel warm like the box had, but felt indifferent like the temperature in the boxcar.

He turned the vial back and forth in his paws, hearing the same faint rattle.

Since there was already something in the vial maybe this task wouldn't take anything from him.

Dusti relaxed his shoulders and curled his paws under his body. He laid his head down on the lukewarm metal floor and listened to the hum of the metal wheels on the train track.

He nodded off to sleep, positive nothing would be taken from him this time, except the vial. And that was definitely something he could live without.

CHAPTER SEVENTEEN
MISS MUFFET

Thick, heavy diesel fumes drenched the air as the train slowed and came into a train yard. Black fog hung over series of railroad tracks crisscrossing through the yard.

An abrasive whistle blew through the fog.

The train jerked, swayed, and jolted across various tracks until finally stopping amid a mass of different train cars.

"What do we do now?" Timber asked.

"Wait here," Dusti said. "And hope we . . . move again."

A loud clicking like a giant ratchet twisted against the front of Dusti and Timber's boxcar. A thunderous clink and an air ripping *POO-OO-SH* blasted from the front as if a bullet was separating the air.

"That's our cue to move," Timber said jumping out of the boxcar.

Dusti followed and glanced at a crane's long cable dangling beside the boxcar. A thick steel pin hung from the crane's hook, separating their boxcar from the other train cars.

Timber looked at the trains sitting on the chaotic railroads splitting out in different directions. "Which one do we take?"

"One going . . . east or south," Dusti said.

"No, not south," Timber said. "The middle of the riddle says, "*When you see where Magnolias grow, remember east is not the way to go.*"According to that we only go south where Magnolias grow."

The tracks vibrated as another boxcar cascaded toward their boxcar. An earsplitting *BOO-OO-OOM* banged from the boxcars as they crashed into each other.

Dusti and Timber jumped.

"Our cue to . . . move again," Dusti said.

"Yep," Timber said. "I wish our cues didn't have to be so loud."

They trotted through the twisted and crossed tracks, dodging rolling boxcars, weaving around coal hoppers, and sneaking under round tank cars.

The afternoon sun glared through the thick black fog as the wind beat through the yard. Two main tracks separated to the east and south at the end of the hubbub of rail. A train of flatcars sat on an eastern track while a train of hoppers rested on a southern track. Steel pipes stretched across a flatcar, bounded tightly with heavy chains. A rich smell of grain drifted from the hopper.

"Which one, Timber?" Dusti asked. "South or east?"

"East," Timber said. "Don't you listen to anything I

say? Hop on the flatcar and hide in the pipes. They'll protect us from birds and other winged creatures."

Dusti squeezed his face into a noncommittal scowl, searching his mind for the good redeeming qualities of Timber. He hopped onto the flatcar, crawled into a bottom pipe, and scurried to the other end.

Timber's claws scraped against the steel pipe as she crawled up behind Dusti.

The wind beat hard against the train as it traveled across Nebraska. The pipes jostled. They grated against the chain, metal scraping metal.

"The train should stop when it's so windy," Timber said.

"The wind's only forty miles an hour," a tiny, high voice said above Dusti.

Dusti looked up. A tangled web canopied over the top of the pipe's opening. A gray spider descended down. Her back comb-footed feet climbed down the string.

Dusti backed into Timber's face.

"I'm right behind you, Dust," Timber said.

"Back up," Dusti said. "There's a poisonous spider . . . in front of me."

"Muffet is poisonous," the spider said nodding her head, "but Muffet only poisons insects. Muffet would never poison a cat. Don't worry."

"She's a comb-foot . . . spider," Dusti said. "The worst kind."

"Muffet is only a common house spider. You're confusing Muffet with her cousin, Black Widow. Black Widow's very poisonous. Stay away from her."

A huge gust of wind blew against the train. The pipes pushed against the chain trying to escape their bounds.

Dusti's fur on his spine rose.

"Don't worry, kitty," the spider said. "The train always stops when the wind's fifty-five miles per hour or when there's a funnel cloud."

The train slowed.

Dusti crawled forward. He peeked out of the pipe.

A train waited on the other track. The suffocating scent of black dust wafted from its coal filled hoppers.

"Why isn't that," Dusti said, "train moving . . . little Miss Muffet?"

Muffet scurried up her web. "That train has to wait on the siding so we don't crash into each other. Hold on tight. Frogs bounce you all around."

A steel X embedded the rails.

Dusti clung to the edge of the pipe as the wheels jerked into the X. The pipes rippled. The vial clunked on his chest.

Dusti glanced at Muffet clinging to her web. "The steel X . . . is a frog?"

"Yes," Muffet smiled and nodded.

"What else do you know . . . about the railroad?"

"Everything."

"Tell us about them," Dusti said. "Please. What's a short line?"

"A short line is a shorter section of track," Miss Muffet said.

She stretched out comfortably in her web, holding up her head with her two front legs. She spent the next eight hours teaching Dusti and Timber all she knew about trains and railroads. She included great men of the railroads past like Casey Jones, railroad's greatest engineer, who gave his life to save all the passengers on his train.

While Muffet talked, the prairie's grave wind grew darker and faster every hour.

CHAPTER EIGHTEEN
THE STORM

An inky night sky enfolded the prairie as the train blew past a number of stations. Loud massive thunder rolled across the sky, shaking the ground. The wind lashed against the flat cars. The train careened. The foreboding smell of destruction and decay pelted the wind and thunder.

Houses, barns, pastures, corrals, and fields of corn, wheat, and hay peppered the prairie as the train wheels grinded to a halt in mid track.

"The wind is stronger," Muffet said sniffing the air.

Dusti wormed out of the pipe. "It smells like . . . destruction. We need to warn everyone. Come on, Tim."

Dusti ambled after Timber as she ran through the fields crying a loud warning at every window.

People ran to their cellars in bathrobes. Flashlights glowed through the windows of basements.

Timber ran to a single wide trailer. She cried, but no one came out.

The wind picked up speed.

"RUN FOR THE . . . DITCH," Dusti yelled over the wind. He reached his head down to his chest and grabbed the vial, holding it in his teeth.

Dusti and Timber fell into a soggy ditch as a funnel cloud surged out of the darkness.

A young lady ran out of the trailer, holding a bundle of yellow material against her chest and a bag looped around her arm as if saving her favorite clothes. Her brown hair thrashed as she fought against the wind.

Dusti shook his head in disgust. How could someone be willing to jeopardize their life for material possessions that could be replaced?

The funnel cloud beaded closer to the ground and ripped though a farm. Corn stalks, grain, and silage flew overhead. Wood, siding, bricks, and glass slashed through the sky.

Dusti cuffed his legs around Timber's head. The loud shredding of fields, the crumbling of houses and the scared screams of cattle tore through the night; and then silence.

"Are you okay?" Dusti asked nudging Timber.

Tears poured out of Timber's eyes. "Let's get back to the train. We did all we could do."

Dusti and Timber crawled out of the ditch dripping with wet sludge.

Houses crumbled around them. The single wide trailer lay on its side. Barns had become splinters. Farms looked like wastelands.

A faint cry shattered the silence.

Dusti crept up the ditch bank towards the cry.

A baby wrapped in a yellow blanket lay sheltered in the marshy ditch. A set of five thin, deep punctures dug into both sides of the ditch bank above the baby's head while below the baby's feet two round holes gripped the sides of the ditch as if protecting the baby from the storm. A bag covered with soft cartoon elephants sat beside the baby.

Dusti searched around the ditch. About ten yards away the young lady with brown hair lay on her back.

"Tim," Dusti said, "check on the lady. See if she's breathing." He hopped into the ditch next to the baby.

"Dust," Timber said, "the train."

"This lady tried so hard . . . to save her baby. I won't let her lose . . . the one material possession . . . she could never replace."

CHAPTER NINETEEN
WRECKAGE

Warm breath rippled out of the baby's nose. His strong legs and arms beat against the blanket while whimpers that carried the scent of mother's milk droned from his mouth. His dark brown eyes darted around as if searching for his mother.

The wet, mushy ditch squelched around Dusti as he noodgied the baby's soft cheek. He lay beside the baby away from his mouth and nose and burrowed his forepaws under the baby's head, keeping it off the wet ground.

Dusti paced his rapid breath and purred a gentle lullaby. Body heat radiated off his warmer body onto the baby's.

The baby's whimpers disappeared into soft, bumbling snores.

Timber ran back to the ditch. She gulped as if swallowing tears. "The lady is breathing, but there's a deep cut on her forehead. I don't know how to stop the bleeding."

Dusti closed his eyes. "Patricia put tissue . . . on Ryan's cuts. See what's in the bag."

Timber's body shook as if in shock. She looped a

canine tooth into the zipper and tore it open. "There are blankets, baby clothes, diapers, and a wallet in here."

"Get a diaper," Dusti said.

Timber pulled a thick disposable diaper out of the bag. She crumpled to the ground. Tears streamed out of her eyes. "I can't do this."

"Sure you can, Tim."

"No, I can't. I'm a cat, not a human. I'm not like you, Dusti. I can't save people. I don't know how."

Dusti wiggled his paws out from under the baby's head and laid it tenderly on the wet ground. "Watch the baby. Lie beside him. Stay away from his . . . mouth and nose. Hold his head off . . . the ground. Don't knead. Purr for him. He likes that."

Timber nodded. She cuddled next to the baby and slid her forepaws, pads down, under the baby's head.

Dusti grabbed the diaper in his mouth and stumbled to the mother.

Dust, sheaths of corn, and bits of grain covered the mother. The knees of her blue jeans were caked with mud. Dirt dug into her fingernails. A deep gash sliced across her forehead as if a board or glass had hit her.

Dusti licked the cut, checking for debris. Then he covered it with the diaper, holding the diaper firmly with his forepaws.

He noodgied the mom underneath the nose every few minutes to make sure she was still breathing.

Soon people staggered out of their cellars and basements. A loud wail of despair rolled across the prairie.

A person whose house stood as strong as if a funnel cloud had never came hugged a neighbor who stood in front of the rubble that was now her house.

An old farmer bent next to the corpses of his cattle and wept into his folded hands.

A family clung together in a tight group hug as if they were happy they still had each other, even though their house staggered sideways.

A little girl held up a book as if it was the most precious thing on earth.

Dusti and Timber meowed trying to get someone's attention, but nobody heard them. The people were distracted with their own grief from losses or jubilations of what they still had that they couldn't hear the two cats crying out for help.

Dusti swallowed, wetting down his dry throat. He tried meowing again, but seven high flutelike notes interrupted him as if someone had found their old flute.

"Dusti hit the dirt!" Timber screamed. "A bird!"

A bright yellow breasted bird dove at Dusti as if trying to steal the vial. A black V decorated the middle of his breast. Air streamed off of brownish black feathers on his back.

Dusti batted at the bird before it could rip the vial from his shoulders.

The bird shot towards Timber. He landed between Timber and Dusti. His dark black eyes peered at the cats.

"I am a western meadowlark," the bird said. "Remember that." He whistled eight high notes and flew down the field still watching Timber and Dusti with his beady black eyes.

Sirens blared down the dirt roads adjacent to the destroyed houses. A big red truck followed by a white van tumbled down driveways and through fields. Blue, white, and red lights flashed on top of both vehicles.

Men and women piled out of the vehicles checking the victims of the funnel cloud.

Dusti and Timber cried for help. The meadowlark sang his high notes, drowning out Dusti and Timber's meows.

"They can't hear us, Dust," Timber yelled. "We're too far away. We have to get them."

"We can't leave."

"Dusti, we aren't human. We can't save them without human help. I can't feed the baby when it gets hungry and you can't sew up that ladies cut. We need their help."

"What if something happens . . . while we're gone?"

"If we don't get help they'll definitely die, no what ifs about that. Leave the diaper on the mom's head and get someone. I'll watch the mom and baby. Go, Dusti."

Ten flutelike notes rang over the fields as the meadowlark skipped through the sky.

Dusti patted the diaper and then tore through the fields, gasping for breath, the vial beating against his chest.

Nine high notes rang through the sky as glares from two flashlights bumped across the field. A bright yellow breasted bird dove through the darkness, chasing two men in blue blazers toward Dusti. Every time the men stopped the meadowlark swooped down, pecking the men's blue hats as if telling them to go on.

"MOW," Dusti hollered as their bright flashlight shined on his face. He turned around and led the men to the mom.

The men's faces twisted in concern. They knelt next to the mom, checked her breathing, and grabbed her wrist.

Toothy grins spread across both of their faces. One man called someone on a radio while the other gently peeled the diaper away from the mom's forehead.

"MEOW," Timber cried from the ditch.

Dusti ran towards Timber joining in her cries. The meadowlark landed next to them and sang his repertoire of notes until one of the men came over.

The man gasped, bent over, and picked up the small baby.

The baby screamed as he was taken away from the warm cuddles of Timber.

The man laughed so hard he cried. He rocked the little baby in his arms.

A number of men and women rushed through the fields. Two carried a stretcher.

Dusti nudged the diaper bag up onto the ditch bank with the help of Timber and the meadowlark.

A blue blazer man patted Dusti and Timber. A tear leaked out of his eye as a huge smile shattered his face. He took the diaper bag and followed the mom and baby to an emergency vehicle.

"Thanks, Western Meadowlark," Timber said. "We've been told that winged creatures aren't our friends."

"You've got that right," the meadowlark said. "Usually

I'm not a cat's friend, but I can guarantee from now on any meadowlark will be your friend."

The meadowlark shrilled eight notes together and flew away.

"Now," Dusti said, "we can go back . . . to the train. We saved two lives. We've done all . . . we could do."

"We did save them, but what if the train isn't there anymore. What if we saved two people, but ended up sacrificing the United States instead."

"The U.S.A. wouldn't be worth saving . . . if we let others die . . . to achieve our means. If the train isn't there . . . we hop on the next one . . . and continue saving the U.S.A. No what ifs . . . about that."

CHAPTER TWENTY
BETTER OFF

Sunrays glittered through the morning's deep purple clouds as Dusti and Timber haggardly walked through the field back to the railroad.

Timber nudged Dusti with her body.

"What?" Dusti asked.

"Nothing. Just playing." Timber batted his ear and swatted his tail.

"Be careful, Timber."

"Why? I can annoy you forever and you won't do anything. The big bad kitty is scared of physical contact." Timber walked in front of Dusti and swiped him with her tail.

Dusti gulped a breath of air and jumped on Timber. They somersaulted over each other. Panting, Dusti pinned Timber to the ground.

Timber's green eyes sparkled. A smirk twitched her whiskers as if she had won.

"I win, Tim. Not you."

"Not the way I see it. I've broken the big, bad kitty's hard exterior. You're finally my friend and you can't deny it."

Timber kicked Dusti off before he could retaliate and ran as fast as she could to where they had left the train.

The train held tight to the track as if the storm had frightened it into immobility. A blue flag waved in front of the train's locomotive.

Timber jumped onto the flatcar with steel pipes. "Miss Muffet? Are you okay?"

The gray spider shimmied down her dusty, tangled web. A smile stretched from leg to leg. Her black eyes sparkled. "Muffet's happy the funnel cloud didn't eat Dusti and Timber."

"We're glad . . . you're safe, too, Muffet," Dusti said, panting. "Why's the train still here. What does the blue flag mean?"

"The track needs to be safe before they can go. The blue flag means gandy dancers are repairing the track. Why were you gone so long? Muffet was worried."

Dusti and Timber hopped into the pipe and told Muffet all about their night adventures.

"Dusti and Timber are braver than Muffet," the spider said. "Why save strangers?"

"I lost someone once," Dusti said. "No one should have to . . . go through that."

"It's more than that," Timber said. "You save things that aren't in danger of losing anything but a fight, like when you saved Tippy and me. What is it with you and saving?"

Dusti shrugged.

"Come on, Dust. You can't expect a friend to go through a nightmare like a funnel cloud and not tell her where this sense of saving comes from."

Dusti sighed blowing Miss Muffet on her thin spider's thread. He brushed the vial resting on his chest. Timber did so much for him, even when she didn't think she could do anymore. Maybe if she knew about his past, it would help her understand him better.

"I used to live with Ryan," Dusti said. "A human boy I adopted. His dad, Burt, beat him . . . and his mom, Patricia. Sometimes I'd get between . . . Ryan and Burt. Every kick, slap, and even broken bones . . . didn't matter, as long as I kept . . . my Ryan safe."

"Is that why your jaw's crooked?" Timber asked. "Did Burt break your jaw?"

Dusti nodded. "I couldn't protect Patricia. Before my family moved . . . Ryan left me at . . . a stranger's house. I lost my Ryan . . . because I couldn't save . . . his mom."

"Ryan didn't leave you because you couldn't save his mom," Timber said.

Dusti shook his head.

"No, Dusti, listen to me," Timber said. "Every time Burt hurt you, I'm sure it tore Ryan up inside. Leaving you was the only way Ryan could save you."

"I was supposed . . . to save him! Who's saving . . . him now?"

"I don't know. I do know Ryan loved you a lot to leave

you somewhere he knew was safe."

The afternoon sun sparkled above the train as it began its journey across the plains. Dusti watched as the destruction from the funnel cloud faded into the distance. He pawed the vial around his neck, worried the wind he had brought with his last task had caused the funnel cloud.

Yellow grain waved from wheat fields. The syrupy smell of maple drenched the air. Wide green leaves fluttered from a grove of sturdy gray trees.

Nebraska's prairie blurred into a smeared tan and gold collage. Dusti didn't have enough energy to pay attention to where he was going anymore. The storm, Timber's friendship, and memories from his past had drained him, leaving a throbbing echo of destruction in their wake.

Dusti stuck his head out of the steel pipe. A cool breeze flickered through his whiskers. He breathed in a long deep breath, thankful the wind had died down to a gentle lull.

Tippy's words beaded through his mind as if carried on the wind. "... *no matter what happens ... no matter what you see, you will finish this task and return to me.*"

Dusti shrank back into the pipe. He held the vial to his chest.

Maybe he hadn't caused the storm with his last task. Maybe Tippy had known the storm would happen and was something Dusti needed to experience to give him more reason, more gumption to finish his quest.

How, though, could he have relied on Timber so heavily during the storm that he let his guard down afterwards?

Now it was just a matter of time before Timber realized she'd be better off without him.

CHAPTER TWENTY-ONE
SAFE

Three long toots blew from the train as it rolled into a city's terminal. Grain elevators reached high into the sky.

Dusti squirmed out of the pipe and sat on the edge of the flatcar as the train rumbled slowly through the terminal, bouncing in and out of crossovers.

The tracks shot straight east after the terminal, but the train didn't pick up speed. It crept slowly across the track as if readying for a switch.

Dusti gripped the edge of the flatcar and searched the tracks in the distance. The railroad split into a Y to the northeast and southeast up ahead.

The train swayed as it clanged into the switch and turned to the northeast.

"Time to go, Tim," Dusti said.

Timber hopped out of the pipe and looked at the fast moving ground. "How do we do this?"

"Jump," Dusti said, "before the train . . . picks up speed."

Dusti jumped off the moving train. His pads shredded across the sandpapery ground as he tried to catch himself and continue running at the same time.

"Good-bye, Miss Muffet," Timber said, leaping off the train.

Muffet waved from the pipe as the train clattered away. "Good-bye kitties. Good luck on your journey and beware of black widows."

The train disappeared to the north leaving Timber and Dusti alone.

Dusti walked in a circle, searching the northern and southern tracks.

"What are you looking for?" Timber asked.

"Magnolias . . . or an eastern track. I can't find either. Hmm, which way . . . do we go?"

"Southeast."

"We can't go south . . . until we see magnolias. Where are . . . the magnolias?"

"We're not going south. We're going southeast."

"Can't you admit . . . you were wrong?"

"I'm never wrong, just a little off sometimes."

Timber stretched asleep on the track while Dusti anxiously paced away the hours searching for a train. He walked across the track as if it was a fence he was prowling.

The tracks vibrated, tickling Dusti's paws. "Come on, Tim. A train's coming."

Timber jumped off the track and crouched with Dusti by the southern track. A black locomotive meandered down the railroad, sashayed into the switch, and lurched toward the south.

A group of rectangular enclosed hopper cars followed the locomotive. A flatcar hauling a long yellow steel beam swayed between two hoppers.

Timber and Dusti ran beside the track. They sprang in the air as the flatcar swished by.

Dusti skidded across the flatcar. His head smacked into the hard yellow beam.

"MEOW," Timber hollered. Her orange forepaws gripped the side of the train. Her claws dug into the metal edge. Her body swayed over the side.

Dusti ran over. Wrenching his hind claws into the flatcar, he bit the scruff of Timber's neck and jerked her onto the train.

Timber tumbled over Dusti. She landed on top of his stomach and buried her head into his neck. "I was so scared. I couldn't hold on. I thought I'd fall on the rails for sure."

Dusti panted. He patted Timber's back. What would he do if he lost her?

Timber's wet tears drenched his chest.

Dusti stiffened his body. He rolled over, sliding Timber off his stomach. He walked as far away from her as he could get. "Remember the rules," he muttered to himself.

"The rules?" Timber asked. "I about die and all you can say is, 'remember the rules'."

Dusti blinked back tears that betrayed his true feelings. "It's over now, Tim. You're safe. That's all that matters."

CHAPTER TWENTY-TWO
REJECTION

Days of silence passed as Dusti and Timber rode south through Kansas' and Missouri's plains, jumping from train to train. Getting on and off the moving trains grew easier the more they did it. Each train they jumped onto carried the same orange emblem stamped across its sides.

Rain poured in sheets as the train zigzagged southeast. A thick fog hung among the mountainous hills of the Ozarks. Oak and hickory trees swelled through the fog. Their green leaves glistened with rain. The sodden brown soil gushed under the trees into a swampy marsh.

Dusti and Timber hid in the confines of a boxcar in op- posite corners as rain beat a calming scent of growth through Arkansas' hills and into the tree filled plains.

Dusti huddled in his lonely corner. He looked at Timber's small orange body curled into a ball as she dili- gently watched out the boxcar's door. Her eyes narrowed as if deep in thought.

Dusti wondered what she was thinking and was about to

ask, but caught himself before any words left his mouth.

The distance that had grown between them since Timber's near death experience, would leave them both happier in the end, even if it made him miserable now.

The train slowed as it entered Tennessee. It crept across a bridge spanning the wide width of the Mississippi River. The river surged through the pounding rain, crawling closer and closer to the crest of the riverbank. Long, flat barges rocked against the mounting river.

A huge city swelled on the other side of the river. Highways wound over each other in a jumbled mess. Vehicles plowed through rain puddles on the highways. Billboards of singers, casinos, and amusement parks bombarded the roadsides.

Dusti looked towards the river. How much more rain could the river handle before it overturned its banks and destroyed this city and countless others?

Irony swathed the United States. The western states were parched, desperately pleading for water and the southeast flooded with water longing for a break in rain.

A mixture of diesel and coal impeded the air as the train swung over crossovers into a loud train hump yard. Large, boxed cranes stretched over rows of tracks. Their metal frames glided down the tracks and picked up train cars as if they were as light as a feather. The train car dangled in the air as the crane moved to another track and lowered the train car onto it.

A switch engine pushed train cars up a single tracked hill. One by one the cars slid down the other side of the hill and onto various tracks like gravity was telling them where to go. A resounding *BOOM* echoed as cars bashed into others already stopped.

Dusti and Timber hopped out of their boxcar before experiencing the hill or crane.

Rain splattered their fur as they searched for a southern or eastern track. Dusti held the vial under his chin protecting it from the rain.

A three-leveled rack train car rested on a southeastern track. Thick metal bars embraced the rack car, concealing new street vehicles stacked across it.

Dusti and Timber ducked between the metal bars and hid from the rain underneath a street car on the lowest level.

Thick haze covered the sky. Night engulfed the hump yard. The train cars crashed throughout the night as if they had no sense of time.

Timber sat as far away from Dusti as she could get. She lay down alone on the damp rack car, curling her tail tightly around her body, concealing as much body heat as possible. Her body shook in uncontrollable shivers. A gentle snore hummed from her nose.

Dusti's empty stomach growled. He rested his head on his paws and watched Timber, wishing he could provide her with extra body heat, but knowing the closer they got the more it would hurt when she left him. The rules were necessary to keep the distance.

But the silence hurt almost as bad as if Timber had already left him. It had made the long train ride excruciatingly more tedious and boring.

Just because he couldn't knead, purr, cuddle, or noodgie Timber, didn't mean he couldn't talk to her.

The train wheels squealed into motion as a gray morning dawned across the train yard.

Timber stretched awake. She sat by a pool of rainwater that had gathered by a car tire. Her pink tongue flicked the water into her mouth.

The train cascaded down the tracks into Mississippi. A valley of pine trees stretched along both sides of the train. The pines reached high in the sky and grew thick together.

Dusti's stomach rumbled as the rain's scent changed from a clean, pure, undiluted smell into the heavenly smell of raw fish.

Short, bushy magnolia trees blossomed along the streets and sidewalks as the train chugged into a town. The trees' green leaves framed gorgeous white magnolia flowers.

An empty classification yard emerged behind the magnolias. Vacant railroad tracks crisscrossed over each other. Stark, silence hung over the yard as if it was hallowed ground.

The train crept slowly passed the yard. The wheels rolled smoothly along the tracks as if afraid to dishonor the past. It clicked as quietly as it could into a switch that split the railroad to the east and south, and continued on its eastward journey.

Dusti rested his paw on Timber's shoulder. "Which way, Tim? East or south?"

Timber rolled her shoulder away from Dusti and jumped off the train.

Dusti dove after her. "Don't be mad. I was joking."

"I'm not mad," Timber said. "I'm remembering the rules, like you told me."

"I wasn't telling you. I was telling . . . myself."

"Right. That makes everything better. It feels wonderful to mean so little to someone."

"It's not that way. You mean a lot to me . . . too much in fact."

"Really? Usually when someone means so-o much to you, you treat them with respect; you treat them as a friend. You may even love them."

Timber turned away from Dusti, splashed through a rain puddle, and walked into the empty train yard.

CHAPTER TWENTY-THREE
CLOUDY FLATCARS

Hours sifted through the pouring rain. Every orange emblem train that chugged passed the vacant yard brought a ray of hope to the drenched cats, until each one shot onto the eastern track, leaving Timber and Dusti cold and abandoned.

Dusti slouched in a rain puddle. His whiskers drooped heavy with rain. Shivering, he panted for breath. He uselessly shook his saturated fur as the downpour soaked into his skin.

An orange emblem train carrying piggyback flatcars, boxcars, and hoppers swooped across the tracks from the eastern railroad.

Dusti sprang from his puddle as the locomotive's wheels juggled into the switch and turned south. He ran with Timber alongside a piggyback flatcar hauling a semi trailer and leaped onto the flatcar before the train picked up speed.

Dusti scooted next to the semi trailer. He felt as if he would never be dry again. The wet stole his warmth, dryness, and even the little breath he had left. Between pants he cleaned his coat with his warm tongue, trying to dig the coldness out of his bones.

Timber snuggled her warm body next to him.

Dusti squirmed away.

"I'm not being affectionate," Timber said looping her paw around him and digging her claws into the side of his stomach. "I don't need your affection, Dusti."

"You needed it," Dusti said, "when I saved your life."

"No, I needed your sympathy, then. And now we need each other's warmth. You're cold and I'm freezing. We need to use our body heat to warm up, just like we did with the baby. Don't worry, I remember the rules— no noodgies, no kneading, and I'm only cuddling for warmth."

Timber's claws slid out of Dusti's stomach. Her cozy fur cuddled against him like a thick winter blanket.

Dusti's bones thawed as he cuddled into Timber. He gulped a purr creeping up his throat. He clasped his paws against his body.

A gentle hum rattled from the wheels like a soft lullaby.

Dusti's eyes grew heavy.

The wheel's metered rattle and Timber's warm embrace coaxed Dusti into a deep sleep like a hypnotist.

Stretching out his hind legs, Dusti wrapped his forelegs around something warm, a blanket he decided in his half consciousness. His paws kneaded the snug, squishy blanket. He felt warm and fuzzy inside and out, only like a happy content cat could feel. He hadn't felt this good since he had cuddled with Ryan.

Dusti ripped open his eyes. His forelegs wrapped around Timber. His paws kneaded her slick orange fur.

Dusti clenched his paws closed and slid them out from under Timber. He tiptoed to the other side of the flatcar.

The train slithered through sheets of rain into another yard. Empty tracks reached east and west. A silver emblem train stood on a southern track, restricting the way.

Dusti shook Timber awake. "Time to go. The train can't go . . . south anymore."

Dusti and Timber jumped off the train as it turned onto the eastern track.

"Do we go west here?" Dusti asked.

Timber glanced at the tracks. "I don't know. The riddle says, 'Ride the next train; soon its track will be done. Then ride a short line towards the setting sun.' But the southern track isn't done. It keeps going. And the western track doesn't look short at all."

Dusti stared at the silver emblem on the southern train.

"The train emblems . . . are different," Dusti said. "The tracks must belong to . . . different companies. The western track must . . . be a short line."

Timber walked along the western track. "It might be, but it doesn't look like it has been used in years."

Dusti huffed for breath as he walked down the western track. Green grass poked through the railroad's ties. Cotton bloomed along the side.

"You're right," Dusti said. "But this is the . . . way to go. We'll have to walk."

"Can you handle walking?" Timber asked.

Dusti looked at the vial on his chest. He heaved a big breath of air and nodded.

The rain slowed to a gentle patter as Dusti and Timber walked down the western railroad into a thick forest of pine.

Sunset hid behind the trees as the sun sank below the tree line. Thick fog covered the moon and stars, casting a murky night over the forest.

A deep rumble floated down the tracks as if a train was coming.

Dusti climbed onto the long steel rail. He meandered down it waiting to feel the vibration of an oncoming train.

The train rumble grew heavier, but the tracks remained stock-still, not vibrating like they had the other times a train was coming.

A ghostly whistle floated over the railroad, "WHOO-OO."

Dusti jumped away from the tracks as a bright, soft white light impeded the fog, shining across the railroad.

A smoky white train drifted down the tracks.

The locomotive crawled past Dusti and Timber.

An enchantingly peaceful, "Whoo-oo," floated through the forest as a row of cloudy passenger cars followed behind the locomotive.

Looking at each other and nodding, Dusti and Timber skipped alongside the train and hopped into an open passenger car. Their paws floated on the soft cloudy ground as if standing in a sea of cotton.

Dusti rode the ghost train as if chasing a dream, timid and scared he'd never achieve his goal of finding Ryan, but filled with an ironic peace like he was safe for now.

CHAPTER TWENTY-FOUR
DUST

A beautiful lilac dawn flowered above the valley of trees beside the railroad track. Green leafy ivy clung to elm and pine trees, turning the forest into a jungle of green. White cotton scattered across fields like snow dotting the ground.

The train whisked into a farm community's town. Yellow dust sprinkled across cars, streets, and houses like Lightning Pixies had shed their light during the night.

The train slowed beside a refurbished sunshine yellow train depot.

Timber and Dusti jumped off the ghost train. They walked onto a hard paved street and watched as the train rumbled up the track disappearing into the distance, leaving a soft, resolute murmur, "WHOO-OOO".

Used cars cluttered the front of an old dilapidated building to the right of them.

Eight flutelike whistles rang from a car.

"Run, Dusti. A bird," Timber said scurrying down the street.

"It's a western . . . meadowlark," Dusti said. "They're

our friends."

"We're too far south and east for western meadow-larks," Timber said. Her eyes grew as round as saucers as she looked above Dusti's head. "That's not a meadowlark. RUN!"

Dusti glanced up. An ashy gray mockingbird swooped towards his shoulders, mimicking the western meadow-lark's song.

Timber's paw flung at Dusti's head.

Dusti ducked.

The mockingbird bounced down the street.

An army of ashy gray mockingbirds flocked out of the dilapidated building. They whizzed through the air heading straight for Dusti and Timber.

A bird's sharp beak pierced Dusti's back. His claws dug into Dusti's spine. He grabbed the vial's string in his mouth and yanked.

The thin string choked Dusti. He coughed. His head spun.

Dusti scrunched his shoulders. He rolled on his back. "Get off me," he hollered.

"Get off me," the bird mocked flying into the air.

Dusti and Timber staggered down the street. They wove around pecan trees. They darted across a huge grassy yard, ducked behind an oak tree, and hopped into a ditch.

"In here," Timber said, ducking into a culvert that stretched across the road. "You guard this opening, I'll take the other."

Dusti collapsed in the warm steel pipe, trying to catch

his breath. He looked at the vial on his chest. Although a little scratched, the vial hung sturdily from the string.

A swarm of mockingbirds dive bombed the culvert's opening.

Dusti arced his back and hissed, "HHEE."

"HHEE," they said.

Dusti leaped out of the culvert. His chest heaved. He recklessly struck the birds as they plunged around him.

A loud huff gurgled out of the oak tree, scattering the mockingbirds away from the culvert. A round, aged armadillo meandered down the trunk and into the ditch. He huddled into the culvert and glared at Dusti. "Don't ya know it's wrong to hurt a mockingbird?"

"We were . . . protecting ourselves," Dusti said.

A low whistle beaded out of the armadillo's mouth. "That's a new one for Arny the Armadilla. You're confused, son. Cats go after birds, not birds after cats."

"They were coming . . . after us," Dusti said. "They want my vial."

"Them mockingbirds don't give an armadilla's backside for that vial. They only fight if offended. Keep quiet. They'll go away. But always keep a look out. Them mockingbirds never forget an offender."

The armadillo slunk out of the ditch and walked down the road.

Silence filled the culvert as the morning dawdled into the afternoon and then the evening. The mockingbirds grew less profuse, giving up in search of a more fulfilling target, worms.

Flares of small yellow lights flashed across the gray dusk of evening.

Dusti blinked his tired eyes.

Another small yellow flash flared across the yard.

Dusti jumped to his paws. "I've found the Lightning Pixies." He climbed out of the culvert and up the ditch.

Timber followed and gasped as what looked like miniscule light bulbs twinkled across the green grass. Their iridescent wings zoomed past Dusti and Timber as if the cats didn't exist.

"I have something," Dusti said, "to give you."

One Lightning Pixie stopped in midair ahead of Dusti and Timber. Her glowing light flashed erratically. A swarm of Lightning Pixies gathered around her, flashing their own lights. They stretched out in a single file line, through the yard, and across a driveway.

Dusti and Timber followed the string of Lightning Pixies to an old oak tree in the backyard of a red brick house. Mushrooms grew out of the oak tree's trunk as if they were fairy beds. Brown, gritty bark haloed around a hole in the oak tree, high above the ground.

The Lightning Pixies flew into the hole as if expecting Dusti and Timber to join them.

Timber glanced from Dusti's paws to the hole. She scrunched up her face and sauntered over to the tree. "Excuse me, oh noble Lightning Pixies. Dusti can't climb."

Dusti backed up across the yard.

"He doesn't have any front claws," Timber said, "He

can't get up there."

Dusti tore through the yard. He careened above Timber and jumped onto a mushroom growing on the trunk as if it was a footstool. He ran up the tree using his hind legs and claws to boost him towards the hole. A sense of energy and freedom surged through him as if he had his front claws back. He ascended up the gritty bark, jumped into the hole, and fell into the Lightning Pixie's burrow, gulping for air.

The Lightning Pixies' two inch bodies fluttered inside the tree as their spiked, blazing blonde hair flashed sporadically on their head. Their muscular arms waved fresh green leaves over Dusti as he tried to catch his breath.

Timber jumped into the hole, clinging to the rim while Dusti slid out of the way. "Dusti, your climbing was awesome. Did any of you see it?"

Dusti smiled. "It felt like I had . . . my front claws back. The Pigsies were right. I'm having feelings . . . I thought I'd . . . never know again."

An old Lightning Pixie fluttered into the tree. Lines emanated around her mouth as if she never smiled. Her back stretched in perfect posture giving her two inch body the look of a giant.

The Lightning Pixies dropped their leaves and flew to the back of the tree. Their wings locked together on their back. They stood straight with their heads held high, feet together.

Dusti cowered as the old Lightning Pixie flew toward him with a tiny pair of scissors. She cut the string away from Dusti's neck and held the long vial in her hands. She flew to a wooden shelf etched inside the tree and tucked the vial behind a small plastic package.

"Shouldn't you open it?" Dusti asked.

"No," the old Lightning Pixie said. "We don't need the vial, the Cypress Gnomes do. I'll keep the vial safe for the next thirty-six hours and then give it back to you."

The old Lightning Pixie flew to the tree's opening and stared at the red brick house.

A tiny Lightning Pixie with big red glasses fluttered into the tree.

Dusti glanced at Timber who shrugged her shoulders.

"What happens in . . . thirty-six hours?" Dusti asked.

"You'll find the Cypress Gnomes," the old Lightning Pixie said. "That gives you enough time to become friends with the people that live in the red brick house."

"We have to become friends with . . . strangers?" Dusti asked.

"They'we weawwy nice," the tiny Lightning Pixie said.

The old Lightning Pixie's mouth bent into a small smile. She shook her head and pointed at the aligned Lightning Pixies.

"Yes, Ma'am," the tiny Lightning Pixie said. She pushed her glasses up her nose and flew to the other Lightning Pixies. Her wings fluttered as she stood bowlegged next to the aligned fairies.

Dusti drummed his paw on the floor, waiting for further instructions.

Timber peered dumbfounded at the old Lightning Pixie.

"I wouldn't just sit there," the old Lightning Pixie said. "You have less than thirty-six hours to make friends with a stranger."

"That's it?" Dusti asked. "No special instructions. No rhyming riddle."

"Here's a rhyme for you," the old Lightning Pixie said. "That's it. It's time to go. Get yourself out of my home."

Dusti and Timber scurried to the tree's opening. Dusti backed out of the tree's hole, gripping the rough bark with his hind claws. He hugged the tree's trunk with his front legs and shimmied to the ground like a koala bear.

Batting through the short tangles of grass, Dusti walked around the house and crept under the holly bushes guarding the front porch. Now instead of being one step closer to Ryan he was at least two steps further away.

CHAPTER TWENTY-FIVE
FRIENDS

A dark, starless sky submerged the trees in night. Hot, humid air enclosed around Dusti and stuck in his throat.

Lights glowed through the windows of the red brick house.

"How do we do this?" Timber asked.

Dusti shrugged and jumped onto the porch. He crawled past a barbeque grill and listened at the doorway.

A boy's cracked laugh rang from the front room, but was soon drowned out by a grown man's deep laughing grumble.

A woman's light, demanding voice broke through the laughter.

The lights clicked off. The pounding sound of running drifted into the back of the house. Silence hung on the porch.

"They sound like a loving family," Timber said snuggling next to the barbeque grill.

Dusti groaned inwardly.

"Dust," Timber asked, "is it possible to make friends in less than thirty-six hours?"

"Sure. You became Tom's friend . . . in less than two minutes."

"I'm not asking about me. I'm asking about you. I've known you for days and you've only teased me with the facade of friendship. You're not my friend yet."

"Yet? Still holding out hope?"

"I always get what I want sooner or later. I got you to talk to me again, didn't I?"

"You were giving me . . . the silent treatment."

"And you broke down and talked to me first. I have you licked."

"If that's what you think."

"I know I have you licked. Right now you can't bear to be without my company and soon you'll be longing for my friendship."

Timber sauntered over to Dusti. She bent towards him as if to give him a noodgie.

Her long pink tongue swiped his cheek. "Consider yourself officially licked."

Dusti wiped Timber's drool off his cheek as she bedded down by the barbeque grill.

"Goodnight, Dusti. Get some sleep. Don't worry about the task. Queen Pigsie said she wouldn't give you anything you can't handle."

Dusti furrowed his lips. Queen Pigsie didn't give him the task to make friends with strangers, the Lightning Pixies had. And thinking back on the old Lightning Pixie's demeanor, he wasn't too sure she had his best interest in mind.

How could he let his guard down enough to become friends with strangers? How could he let someone into his life that would be gone in a couple of days? What if the man was the same kind of lowlife as Burt? Would he ever complete this task and see Ryan again? Or was he permanently stuck with Timber by his side?

Dusti breathed in the sticky air. The last alternative didn't sound too bad. Timber could be permanently stuck by his side as long as Ryan was right there with them.

A bright yellow light blared through the front window's curtains as a hazy dawn drifted over the trees. The grainy smell of grits snuck out of every crack in the house.

A soft padding neared the door.

Dusti hid by Timber under the holly bushes as the lock on the door clicked.

A lady pulled the door open and wandered out to her car, leaving the door cracked.

Dusti and Timber pelted for the door and pushed it open enough to creep through. They slid inside the cool house.

Dark wicker baskets framed the living room's soft maroon carpet.

"AH-AH-AH-CHOO," exploded from a room near the back of the house.

Timber and Dusti sprang down the hall and slid into the nearest bedroom.

Dusti peered in the closet. Blue jeans, t-shirts, and

cowboy boots cluttered inside; books stood astutely on the shelves.

The smell of cinnamon wafted from the bed, coaxing Dusti closer.

Dusti pattered cautiously to the bed.

The smell of cinnamon grew stronger flanking the room's musty odor of high humidity.

Lightly jumping up on the bed, Dusti climbed over the mound of a person wrapped up in blankets.

The warm smell of cinnamon swarmed around the body.

"Mow?" Dusti asked, pawing at the covers.

An older boy pulled the covers off of his face. A halo of curly, honey blonde hair feathered around his head. He blinked and rubbed his baby blue eyes, trying to focus.

"Dusti?" the boy asked.

CHAPTER TWENTY-SIX
SILVER HEART

Dusti clenched and unclenched his paws in an ongoing knead. He rubbed his scent glands across the kid's face and noodgied his warm, three-freckled nose.

Timber quietly hopped up on the bed.

"Timber," Dusti said, "We've found . . . Ryan."

Ryan's warm hand caressed Dusti's back.

A loud purr erupted from Dusti's mouth. He gratefully kneaded Ryan's chest, forgetting about everything else. Finally he was home.

"AAH-AAH-CHOO," exploded from the hallway.

The lady ran past Ryan's door with a box of tissue and medicine and glanced inside.

Stopping in her tracks, she marched into Ryan's room. She looked from Dusti to Timber. Her eyes narrowed as her hands flew up to her sides. "Ryan!"

Ryan shook his head. He clutched Timber and Dusti tight to his body. "Dusti," he said.

Patricia walked to the bed. She squinted at Dusti's

broken jaw.

Dusti wriggled out of Ryan's grasp. He noodgied Patricia's arm and held his spiraled tail high as he walked back and forth in front of her.

A gentle laugh like the tinkle of wind chimes jangled from Patricia's mouth.

"AH-AH-CHOO," exploded from the hallway.

Patricia laid the medicine and tissue on the bed. She walked over to a picture of a small grayish brown kitten hanging on the wall. A collar with a silver heart dangled on the picture's wooden frame. Unhooking the collar, she set it next to Ryan. She stroked both cats' backs and pointed towards Ryan's window as if she wanted them outside.

Ryan grabbed the collar. He looped it around Dusti's neck and snapped it into its latch.

Dusti held his head high as the silver heart dangled on his chest.

Ryan bundled Dusti and Timber outside and soon served them an elegant meal of tuna, roast chicken, and water.

Dusti's silver heart jingled every time it hit the side of the water bowl or food plate, reminding him he was home.

"AH-AH-CHOO," sprang from the doorway as Patricia and Burt walked through.

Dusti squinted at the backside of Burt as he ambled into the driveway. He wore tan coveralls over a green shirt. His brown hair had now faded to gray.

Patricia rubbed his back as she followed him outside in a raggedy jogging suit. Her hair was thrown up helter-skelter in a ponytail on top of her head.

Burt and Patricia hugged before he got in the full-sized green truck. Patricia stood in the driveway waving and blowing kisses as he backed out and went down the road.

Dusti lay down and held his paws on his forehead.

"What's wrong?" Timber asked.

"Nothing makes sense. Burt has changed. He wouldn't let . . . Patricia near him . . . if she wasn't dressed up. Patricia and Ryan seem . . . happy."

"And this is a bad thing?"

"No. But how can I . . . be friends with . . . someone I can . . . never forgive?"

"You don't need to be friends with Burt," Timber said, "no matter what the Lightning Pixies say. But you do need to forgive him."

Dusti growled.

"No, Dust, listen to me. The reason to forgive others is to help yourself. Forgiving doesn't mean you accept or are okay with what someone else has done. It just means you won't let their mistakes and bad behavior control your thoughts. It's a way to free yourself from their control."

Dusti dropped his paws to the ground contemplating what Timber had said. It made sense. He didn't want to live his life bogged down with hateful memories of unkind actions. He wanted to be free and happy.

Dusti smiled as a smell of minty toothpaste floated through the front door.

Ryan bounded out and grabbed Dusti in his arms. He petted and squeezed him, speaking human words Dusti couldn't understand, but was sure he agreed with.

Ryan put Dusti down, patted Timber between the ears, and raced into the backyard. He swung his hand forward, motioning Dusti and Timber to follow him.

Dusti sprang after him gasping for breath.

Timber sat timidly on the porch.

"Come on, Tim," Dusti said. "Ryan wants to play . . . with us."

Timber giggled and bounded after Dusti.

The morning sun twinkled through the oak, pine, and pecan trees in the backyard. Ryan snatched a stick out of the garden and waved it back and forth.

Dusti crouched down on the dewy grass. His eyes followed the malicious stick. He shook his haunches and darted at the stick, grabbing it in his paws, struggling for breath. He rolled over, gripped it in his teeth, and beat the stick with his back legs, gulping the humid confining air between kicks.

A deep, squeaky laugh rolled out of Ryan's mouth. Crooked grown-up teeth gleamed as a huge jack-o-lantern smile covered Ryan's face.

Dusti felt like he was glowing from the inside out. Before Ryan had rarely laughed or smiled as if he was afraid to make too much noise or show too much pleasure. Now his laughter rang from the treetops. His face glimmered in a hearty smile.

Timber hid behind rose bushes framing the house as Ryan and Dusti played.

Dusti was having too much fun to worry about Timber's

pouting and soon forgot about her. The backyard had become his oasis. He spent the morning and afternoon playing with Ryan trying to reclaim at least some of the time Ryan and him had lost.

"Ryan," a gruff voice hollered from the side yard. A man wearing brown coveralls ran into the backyard. His brown eyes twinkled.

Ryan carried Dusti over. "Dusti," Ryan said. He pointed at the man, "Shane . . . Dad."

A crooked smile radiated across Shane's tan face. "AH-AH-CHOO," he sneezed. His eyes grew puffy, but twinkled even through their puffiness. He bent down and scratched Dusti between the ears.

"AH-AH-CHOO," he sneezed, spraying Dusti with saliva.

Ryan laid Dusti on the grass and led Shane inside their house.

Dusti peered after Shane and Ryan, relieved Burt was no longer in the picture, but worried just the same.

Shane seemed like an okay guy, but first impressions could be deceiving. Could Dusti trust Shane? Did he take care of Dusti's family? Did he love Ryan and Patricia unconditionally?

Dusti snuggled in the long grass as trust and friendship issues tormented his mind.

Inhaling a stiff breath of sultry air, Dusti hoped he could learn to trust the unknown in less than eighteen hours and become friends with a perfect stranger by tomorrow morning.

CHAPTER TWENTY-SEVEN
PERFECT STRANGER

Lightning Pixies glittered across the backyard as the sun faded behind the tall, profuse trees. Ryan and his new dad threw a football back and forth while Patricia relaxed in a lawn chair, cheering them on.

Dusti cuddled in Patricia's warm, soft lap, closely observing Shane. He kneaded Patricia's cotton t-shirt and noodgied her hand whenever it got close enough to his nose. He breathed quietly trying his hardest not to gasp.

Timber wandered around the backyard as if she didn't know where she belonged.

"Here kitty, kitty," Patricia said.

Dusti stood on Patricia's chest and noodgied her under the nose.

A laugh tinkled from her mouth. "No, Dusti," she said pushing him to the side of her lap. She motioned at Timber and patted the side of the chair. "Here kitty, kitty."

Timber darted over and jumped in Patricia's lap. She rubbed her scent glands on Patricia's hand. A thunderous purr rumbled out of her mouth. She kneaded Patricia's jean shorts as if she had been missing affection as much as Dusti had.

"Timber?" Patricia asked looking closely at Timber's ginger fur.

Timber noodgied Patricia's arm.

"Dusti and Timber," Patricia said. She shook her head and giggled, "Tom."

As the last light of evening faded into darkness, Ryan and Shane came over to Patricia. Shane helped Patricia up while Ryan grabbed the cats from her lap.

Shane bent over to give the cats a love pat, but Patricia pushed him away.

Shane nodded. He wrapped Patricia in a tight hug and gave her a light kiss. As he let Patricia go, he quickly petted the cats.

Patricia frowned and shook her finger at him.

Shane shrugged. Looping his arm through Ryan's and holding Patricia's hand, they walked together back to the front of their house.

Dusti and Timber followed them to the front porch and bedded into oval wicker baskets Shane had set out for them.

Dusti snuggled into his basket as the air wrapped around him like a warm quilt.

Lightning zigzagged through the trees. Large raindrops flooded the sky, pounding on the roof of the covered porch. Pecans pitter-pattered onto the sidewalk falling from the trees. A homey smell of fish rolled off the puddles surging around the carport and lawn.

Dusti grinned. Ryan's life was perfect now. He had a new dad that loved him, made him happy, and would never lay a hand on him.

Dusti couldn't stop smiling as he fell into a heavy sleep.

A faint buzz trembled around Dusti. His ears tickled as if spider legs were crawling inside.

"Dusti, wake up." The buzzing sound increased. A sharp tugging pulled on his ears.

Dusti blinked his eyes open. Fog floated above the drenched lawn. The soft glow of streetlights glimmered in the predawn haze. Small flares of light flickered across the porch.

Stretching awake, Dusti curled his back and yawned.

"Don't gobbow us up, Dusti," the tiny Lightning Pixie said. Her hair flickered like a string of Christmas lights. She shifted her red round glasses up her nose.

The old Lightning Pixie flew towards Dusti. She held the vial in her small hands as if it weighed nothing and tied it under his chin. "Ryan and Shane will go to Noxubee Wildlife Refuge today. Go with them, but don't let them see you. There you'll find the Cypress Gnomes. Give them the vial."

"I've seen Ryan . . . for one day," Dusti said. "Now I have to have him . . . taken away?"

The old Lightning Pixie shook her head. "Clearly, you have more lessons to learn. Complete this task, and then you may return. Sleep now. Be well rested for the task ahead."

The old Lightning Pixie turned sharply and flew as far away as she could get.

"Wait," Dusti said. "Where are the . . . Cypress Gnomes?"

A soft melody hummed through the darkness.

Timber stretched awake.

A group of Lightning Pixies buzzed above Dusti and sang, "Deep in the swamp Cypress Gnomes lie, past the American Lotus are where they hide. Disappearing amongst the trees, they hide everything from sight but their knobby knees. Though often seen, they're rarely found. Nobody ever finds them standing on the ground."

Dusti closed his eyes and repeated the riddle in his head until he had it memorized.

The tiny Lightning Pixie shifted her glasses up her nose and flew in front of Dusti. "In da swamp, bewawe of da bwack wiwwow. She's scawy."

"So we've heard," Dusti said cuddling back down in his basket.

Timber yawned loudly as the Lightning Pixies flew away. "What's a bwack wiwwow?"

"Black widow," Dusti said. "Remember Muffet's cousin, the black widow spider."

"Oh, yeah," Timber said. "Are you scared of this next task, Dusti?"

"Nah," Dusti said closing his eyes. And he wasn't. He could handle anything as long as he got to come back home with Ryan.

*   *   *

The clatter of dishes and water rang through the front door as Ryan ambled onto the porch, toting two fishing poles in one hand and an ice chest in the other. He carried the fishing gear to the green truck and tucked them under the toolbox that stretched across the truck's bed.

Dusti held his chin securely over the vial as Ryan came back onto the porch, bent over, and hugged both Timber and him.

Ryan skipped back to the truck as Shane and Patricia hugged each other in the living room.

Dusti and Timber snuck across the lawn to the back of the truck. They jumped into the truck bed, landing as light as a feather and scurried under the toolbox on the driver's side.

"Dust," Timber whispered, "we don't know what'll happen with the Cypress Gnomes, what you'll lose, or if you'll get to see Ryan again. Maybe I should find them by myself, so you can stay with Ryan."

"The Lightning Pixies promised . . . I'd get to come back . . . to Ryan. This time I won't . . . . lose anything. Something's in the vial. Listen."

A faint whisper shifted inside the vial as Dusti pawed it back and forth.

"The only problem is . . . finding the Cypress Gnomes," Dusti said. "I can't find them . . . without you. I need you, Timber."

"You do?"

"Sometimes."

"That's what I thought. You only need me when it's convenient for you."

"That was a joke. You know, ha-ha."

"No, it wasn't. How would you feel if I was only there for you when it was convenient for me? How would you feel if I found a family and forgot all about you?"

"I'm sorry you're jealous."

"I'm not jealous. I'm happy you found Ryan. I really am. I knew this would happen, though, I knew you'd forget about me someday, I just didn't think it would be so soon."

Dusti turned away from Timber. He thought she'd know how important it was for him to spend every second he could with Ryan. He thought she'd be lenient with him for ignoring her, considering the circumstances.

The truck sped away from the house and down a tree lined highway, splashing through puddles that had gathered the night before. Lingering raindrops dripped from the boughs of pine trees huddled together beside the road.

Dusti inhaled the thick waterlogged aroma of pine and rain. Mississippi smelled like home to him.

The masses of pine trees thinned as the truck drove into a town. Grand Antebellum homes flashed along the streets. Wide pillared porches wrapped around the massive houses.

Shane drove through the town's paved streets and onto a dirt county road. Acres of farmland spread across the hills, ending in a refuge of untouched forest.

Slender branches of bushy willow trees scattered

throughout the forest of lakes and swamps. Egrets splashed in the shimmering lake water and fluttered along the green marshes.

Shane stopped the truck alongside a lake covered with American Lotus. Their soft yellow flowers stood like single stemmed roses on top of green lily pads floating on the lakes.

Dusti and Timber scampered out from under the toolbox. They dove out of the truck and ran down the road, hiding behind a tree before Shane or Ryan spotted them.

CHAPTER TWENTY-EIGHT
BWACK WIWWOW

Dusti and Timber trotted past the lake of American Lotus.

Tall, grayish brown cypress trees waded in murky water. Gray Spanish moss draped over the treetops like witch's hair. An aged, pitted boardwalk wove through the trees and deep into the swamp.

Darkness oozed across the rickety boardwalk leading into the swamp. Shrouds of moss floated around thick, grayish brown tree stubs barely peeking above the murky water.

A round green blob swam towards the boardwalk. A curved shell rose out of the water. A green, slimy head exploded out of the shell.

"AAHH," Dusti screamed.

A low garbled noise thudded out of the monster's mouth. He grinned like a grandpa without teeth. "Don't be scared of me. I'm only a turtle."

"Can you help us?" Timber asked. "We're looking for

the Cypress Gnomes. Do you know where we can find them?"

"Cypress Gnomes," the turtle said. He climbed onto a grayish brown tree stub. "These're cypress knees and those're cypress trees," he pointed at the trees draped in moss. "There ain't no Cypress Gnomes. All ya tourists come looking for Cypress Gnomes. I've been in this swamp for dang near ninety years and I ain't never seen no Cypress Gnomes."

The turtle huffed off the cypress knee and dunked back into the water.

"Thanks," Dusti said as the turtle swam away. "That helps a lot."

"Actually it does," Timber said. "The Cypress Gnomes hide everything from sight, but their knobby knees." She knocked on a cypress knee. "Hello, is anyone home?"

"Can it really be . . . a gnome?" Dusti pounded on the cypress knee. "It looks like a tree. It feels like a tree. It even sounds like . . . a tree. Guess what . . . it's a tree."

"Okay, genius. Since you're so smart you figure it out."

Dusti hummed the last lines of the riddle. "Though often seen, they're rarely found. Nobody ever finds them. . . standing on the ground. They must be in . . . the air."

"Of course, flying gnomes. I hear of them every day."

Ignoring Timber, Dusti hopped on the cypress knee. He stared into the branches of the cypress trees, hunting for anything that looked like a gnome.

Bubbles rippled from the swamp. The cypress knee quivered. The earth rumbled.

Dusti grasped onto the cypress knee. "Tim, get out of here. The earth's quaking."

The swamp ripped open. Two great, murky walls of mud and water shot up on either side of the cypress knee.

"NO," Timber said. "You're not going without me." She shot through the swampy wall.

Dusti flung out his paw and cuffed it around her, pulling her onto the knee. Murky, stagnant water dripped from her whiskers as she balanced on her tippy-paws next to Dusti.

Two gnarled boughs wrapped around Dusti and Timber, cupping them to the knee.

The knee jerked Dusti and Timber into the swamp and slid them underground. It glided them through miles of earth with as much agility as a fish swimming in water.

The knee jolted to a stop. Gruff voices pelted out a monotonous working chant synchronized in time to a chinking sound.

The gnarled boughs unwrapped Dusti and Timber into a saturated earthen lair. Water dripped from the ceiling and walls as if they'd soon collapse. Huge pools puddled the ground.

Small, brusque men chipped at the earthen walls with pickaxes. Long, gray beards resembling Spanish moss draped from their faces. Their knotted backs bent forward as if in a permanent stance. They cursed as wet earth dribbled from the walls.

Dusti gulped the heavy, putrid air.

"Dusti," Timber said smacking his back, "this isn't a cypress knee, it's a small man."

Two big green eyes on either side of a twisted nose, stared at the vial around Dusti's neck. A gray beard tickled Dusti's ears.

Dusti slid down the knobby knee into a furrowed lap.

A gnarled hand ripped the vial from Dusti's neck.

"That isn't yours," Dusti said batting the gnarled hand.

A chinging rang through the lair as every small man dropped his pickax. They ran over to Dusti and surrounded him. "Oh yeah, who does it belong to, fur ball?"

"The Cypress Gnomes," Dusti said.

The small man thumped Dusti off his lap and tweaked Timber off his knee. "Who do you think we are? I'm not merely a cypress knee, but the King of the Cypress Gnomes."

He twisted the lid off the vial and peered inside. He stood in the center of his Gnomedom.

"Gnomes," King Cypress Gnome said, "the fur ball with the wretched tail brings the one thing we need more than anything. The one treasure our gnomedom is lacking, the most precious element."

He passed the vial around the circle. "Earth."

King Cypress Gnome poured the earth into his cupped hand. He blew it throughout his Gnomedom.

Dusti's body collapsed as the earth grabbed onto the saturated walls, dripping ceiling, and pools of water. The earth evaporated the water from the ground, desiccated the saturated walls, and ended the ceiling's incessant drip.

The Cypress Gnomes stared at their dry lair. Their mouths twitched almost in a smile.

King Cypress Gnome grabbed Dusti and Timber in his hands. "When you add a solid to a liquid, what happens to the liquid?"

Dusti and Timber shrugged in his tight grasp.

"It rises," he said jumping through the earthen ceiling. He held the cats tightly as he soared through miles of earth and back into the swamp.

The swamp had risen in the short time they had been gone. It ran over the rickety boardwalk covering the edges in mud, water, and slime.

King Cypress Gnome dropped Dusti and Timber on the boardwalk. "Our Gnomedom has what it needs, but it won't balance the United States. The water will continue to rise. Run!"

King Cypress Gnome disappeared under the swamp, sticking out his knee.

Dusti struggled to stand, but his legs wouldn't support him. He stretched his legs out flat and crawled against the boardwalk. He crawled as fast as he could down the middle as the swamp rapidly submerged the boardwalk's sides.

Dusti and Timber scurried onto the road as the boardwalk plunged into the swamp's murky abyss.

A deluge of rain splattered from the sky. It ricocheted across the lake, pelting the American Lotus. A swarm of snowy white egrets hovered into the sky.

Shane's empty truck sat across the road.

"We're almost there," Dusti said crawling toward the truck.

An egret dove, reaching his long pointed talons at Dusti.

"We can't make it," Timber yelled. She pushed Dusti out of the egret's way and into the thin low limbs of a black willow tree. "We'll be safe in here until the egrets go away."

A slithering sound wrapped around the tree. Thin limbs snaked around Dusti and Timber.

"FE-FI-FO-FILLOW," a great roar barked. "WHO DARES DISTURB THE BIG BLACK WILLOW?"

CHAPTER TWENTY-NINE
BONDED PROMISE

The black willow's thin branches wrapped around Dusti and Timber's hind legs and held them tightly to the ground.

An oval wall of limbs fell like a castle gate and dug into the ground, surrounding the cats like prison bars. The willow's thin branches wove around and above Dusti and Timber, interlacing through and back over the vertical limbs into a thick solid nest.

"ROW," Dusti and Timber cried.

Rain swelled across the ground. The lake overwhelmed its banks, spilling across the shore.

"We'll drown if we don't get out of here," Timber said.

"ROW," they shrieked as they dug, scratched, and tore at the black willow's basket.

Splashing bounded across the road. A sharp metallic scratch rang from the truck as if Shane and Ryan were putting away their fishing poles.

"MEOW," Dusti and Timber hollered.

The swing of a door opening rang through the rain.

The tree shook as if laughing to itself.

"MEOW, MEOW," Dusti and Timber screamed.

Water splashed around the tree.

"Kitty?" Shane asked.

"ROW," Dusti cried.

A silver hatchet glowed through the gaps in the basket.

The branch wrapped tighter around Dusti's hind leg. It tugged on him as if trying to hide him away.

Shane chopped the branch that held Dusti's leg. Blood pounded back into his paw.

A rhythmic snapping beat around the willow. The silver hatchet glimmered. Shane chopped the vertical branches with such precision as if he had done this before.

"Meow," Dusti said as Shane lifted off an oval wicker basket.

"Dusti, Timber?" Ryan asked.

Shane nestled Dusti and Timber into the wicker basket, grabbed Ryan's hand, and ran back to the truck. He set the wicker basket in the truck's cab between Ryan and him.

Muddy water splattered across the truck as Shane drove through the refuge with as much speed as a racing pronghorn.

Water dripped from Dusti's whiskers. Mud caked between his pads.

Shane sniffled and grabbed a handkerchief. A loud sneezing fit bombarded the cab of the truck. Shane blew his nose. The skin around his eyes swelled.

Ryan frowned. He looked from the cats to Shane.

Dusti gripped the side of the basket. He needed to get

out and as far away from Shane as possible. He tried pulling himself out, but his back legs crumpled under him.

Ryan's face crinkled around his eyes and on his forehead. A frightened, high-pitched voice warbled from his
mouth. He pulled Dusti out of the basket and stood him on
his lap, but Dusti's legs wilted underneath him.

Shane glanced at Dusti. He talked calmly, ruffled
Ryan's hair, and petted Dusti.

Ryan's tense legs relaxed.

Dusti cuddled onto Ryan's lap. Shane made everything
better. He had saved Timber and him from the black willow, calmed Ryan's fears, and Dusti was positive Shane
would do everything he could to get him walking and maybe even breathing right again.

Large raindrops beat against the windows of Ryan's
warm house for the rest of the day. They slid down the
window and plopped loudly on the ground as if pleading
with Dusti.

Dusti disregarded the rain as Ryan and Patricia dried,
pampered, and cuddled Timber and him inside the dry
house.

As night drifted around the trees, Shane arranged the
cats' wicker baskets in the middle of the living room, tucking feathery towels into them. He laid both cats in the
wicker baskets, constantly blinking his watery eyes and
sniffing his dripping nose.

Dusti nuzzled into the soft downy towel. He glanced at
the wicker baskets lining the walls, stuck into corners, and

adorning shelves; positive each basket had once held a scared animal Shane had saved and doctored.

Dusti's eyes grew heavy. Proud, happy thoughts of being Ryan, Patricia, and Shane's pet danced through his mind and lulled him to sleep like a lullaby.

A relentless clicking woke Dusti in the middle of the night. Blinking his eyes open, he peered into the soft light coming from the dining room.

Shane stood by the table in loose gray shorts and a rumpled white shirt. He dug his finger in his ear while clicking his tongue. His puffy eyes were bloodshot as if he had been rubbing them all night. A watery fluid dripped from his nose and eyes. He snapped the lid off a medicine bottle and took two pills with a glass of water.

Dusti looked at the empty wicker baskets. All the other animals hadn't stayed after Shane had saved them. They respected Shane enough to leave so they didn't upset his allergies anymore.

Dusti snuggled back into his basket. He couldn't leave. He loved Ryan too much.

Shane sniffed. He wiped his raw red nose with a tissue.

Timber hopped out of her basket.

"What are you doing?" Dusti whispered.

"We're making Shane miserable. We need to go outside. There are more important things to care about than your own happiness."

"You're right," Dusti said stumbling out of his basket.

Timber walked to the door. "Mew, mew."

"Mew, mew," Dusti added.

Shane groped into the living room. He picked up Dusti and Timber, opened the door, and set the cats on the porch, smiling through his puffy eyes.

The gentle hum of rain poured from the sky, ending in soft taps as it joined the over flowing puddles on the ground.

Dusti nodded as he lay on the porch. This would work. He didn't have to be a house cat to stay with Ryan. He could live happily outside Ryan's house and Shane wouldn't have to suffer from allergies caused by him anymore.

A series of loud sneezes exploded through the house.

Dusti stared at the closed door. He looked at the heart hanging from his collar, resting on his chest. His head dropped onto the cold cement patio as reality sank in.

He couldn't stay here with Ryan. Every time Ryan petted him, hugged him, or even loved him, his fur and dander would cling to Ryan, get carried inside, and aggravate Shane's allergies. His fur and dander were like poison to Shane.

Patricia and Ryan were finally happy. Shane loved them as much as Dusti did. Shane would do anything for them. He was the best dad Ryan could ever have.

Dusti pounded his front paws on the patio, reprimanding his stingy, selfish love. It was time he loved unselfishly. He needed to take himself out of the equation and think about others.

He wouldn't destroy the happiness that overwhelmed

Ryan, Patricia, and Shane. He had to leave. Ryan had always loved Dusti unselfishly. He had left him once to save him from Burt and give him a better life. Now Dusti could return the favor.

Dusti panted as silent tears streamed down his face. Wiping and swallowing them away, he turned to Timber. "Will you get the . . . Lightning Pixies? It's time to return . . . to Tippy."

"Are you mad?" Timber asked.

"Isn't this what I'm . . . supposed to do?"

"Yes, I'm just wondering why you're doing it. What your intentions are."

"I'm bonded to the promise . . . I made with Tippy."

"Of course, returning to Tippy can't be for unselfish reasons like making Ryan happy or relieving Shane's allergies."

"Timber, just get them . . . please."

Timber nodded and dove into the swamp of water cascading around the porch.

CHAPTER THIRTY
UNSELFISH LOVE

A whimsical buzz flickered through the air. Miniscule lights flashed sporadically as a group of Lightning Pixies fluttered onto the porch.

The old Lightning Pixie flew ahead of the group. She landed before Dusti, tucking her wings behind her back. A smile creased away the scowl lines etched around her lips. "Ryan and Patricia are safe with Shane. They always have been and always will be."

Dusti nodded. "It doesn't make leaving . . . any easier. At least I saw Ryan . . . one more time."

The old Lightning Pixie patted Dusti's paw like a hammer.

"I promised the Great . . . Tippy-Tippy Roo-Roo . . . I'd return to him after . . . I finished my quest. It's time to go home."

The old Lightning Pixie shook her head. She waved the group of Lightning Pixies forward. The tiny Lightning Pixie stood at the head of the group holding a small plastic bag in her hand.

"It's not time to see the Great Tippy Roo-Roo yet," the old Lightning Pixie said.

"It's not?" Dusti asked. "We visited the . . . Cypress Gnomes yesterday."

"I see that," the old Lightning Pixie said, looking at Dusti's dilapidated body. "I'm sure King Cypress Gnome told you the United States isn't balanced yet. There's one more task that needs to be completed."

Dusti slumped onto the porch as if a twenty pound bag of potatoes was thrown on top of him. How could he do another task? He couldn't walk or breathe. He had nothing left to give.

Conflicting thoughts tore their way through Dusti's mind like a rampaging bull. He wanted to save the United States. He wanted to stop disasters from tearing across the land, destroying houses, property, animals, and families. He never wanted anyone to go through the heartache and pain of what he saw in Nebraska, but he couldn't do this anymore.

The old Lightning Pixie grabbed Dusti's chin. Her small fingers pinched his fur and gripped his crooked jaw bone as if digging into the marrow. "If you quit now, your tomorrow, Ryan's tomorrow, my tomorrow, and every-one's tomorrow is limited."

Dusti jerked his chin out of the old Lightning Pixie's tight grasp.

He looked at Timber. She sat resolutely by him like his shadow. She would go anywhere he went. She would bear any burden he had to.

Dusti shook his head. He couldn't keep depending on Timber to live through meaningless disasters, witness unspeakable perils, bear incomprehensible burdens anymore.

The tiny Lightning Pixie fluttered over to Dusti and held out a plastic bag for him. "Pwease, Dusti, we need youw hewp. Youw da onwy one who can do dis. Pwease."

Dusti turned to Timber. The sun's first rays glimmered through the rain shimmering on her bedraggled orange fur like the hues of an angel. She nodded at the tiny Lightning Pixie as if she was Dusti's conscience.

"You don't have to come with me . . . this time, Timber," Dusti said.

"What?" Timber asked. "And let you have all the fun, not a chance, Dusti. I'll be with you forever, there's no getting rid of me. I thought you knew that."

"You'd think by now . . . I would."

Dusti turned to the Lightning Pixies. "What's our next task?"

The Lightning Pixies clasped hands, circled around Dusti and Timber, and danced around them.

The old Lightning Pixie fluttered away from the merriment. Her scowl lines reappeared deeper and more furious than before. She slapped her forehead and shook her head as the Lightning Pixies began chanting.

"Before the Mississippi overflows, ride the Arkansas west toward your home. When you see colors flare across the sky, the United States will be born again and never die."

Dusti nodded, not quite sure what they were talking

about. "How do I get to . . . Arkansas? I can't walk well."

The group of Lightning Pixies split into two groups. They swooped around Dusti and Timber, grabbing at their fur. "We'll carry you of course."

"Wait," Dusti said backing away from the tiny Lightning Pixie and plastic bag. "I need to give Ryan . . . a proper good-bye. I don't want him to . . . worry."

The old Lightning Pixie's scowl lines faded. She fluttered over to Dusti and knocked his jaw with her clenched fist. "I wouldn't have it any other way."

Dusti rubbed his jaw and crawled to the front door. "Tim, are you coming?"

Timber hesitantly marched to the door as if she was dreading the good-bye just as much as him.

"Timber," Dusti said, "Thanks for sticking with me . . . through everything."

"Come on, Dust," Timber said, "stop hesitating. We have to say good-bye. Save your sappiness for Ryan. Don't spend it all on me."

"MEOW," Timber cried.

Dusti inhaled a big gulp of air as the front door opened. Shane stood on the other side.

Dusti mustered all the strength he could to stand on his four legs. He tottered through the doorway, each step harder than the last. He paused next to Shane and noodgied his foot.

Timber darted inside, hopped onto the couch, and into Patricia's lap.

Patricia giggled as Timber noodgied her hand and cheek

over and over again.

Dusti marched slowly and with great effort into Ryan's room. "Mew," he said walking through the doorway.

A huge smile creased Ryan's face. "Dusti."

Dusti rubbed against Ryan's ankles. He looped a paw around his collar and pulled it off.

Ryan shook his head. He picked up Dusti and the collar. He cradled Dusti in his arms and snapped the collar back around his neck. "You're *my* Dusti."

"Meow." Dusti noodgied Ryan. He kneaded his arm. Tears leaked out of his eyes. He wanted so desperately to tell Ryan how much he loved him. He wished he could talk human or Ryan could understand cat. "Meow."

Ryan hugged Dusti, kissed the top of his head, and set him back on the ground.

"Meow," Dusti said. He held his head high and marched out of the room. The silver heart on his collar pattered on his chest, reminding him with every step he would forever be Ryan's Dusti.

"Dusti," Ryan called.

Dusti turned around in the doorway.

"I love you, too."

CHAPTER THIRTY-ONE
COMPASSION AND LOVE

The Lightning Pixies flew hour upon hour, never wavering with their heavy loads. Wet, sultry air pelted Dusti's face. Pine tree branches slumped, laden with the night's heavy rain. The heart on Dusti's collar beat against his neck.

A warm breeze cut through Dusti's whiskers as the Lightning Pixies carried him across the plains. Drenched fields of soybeans and cotton cascaded across the land.

Mississippi's mighty, churning river tore southwards. Its turbulent water escalated towards the banks.

The Lightning Pixies flew into a small Arkansas neighborhood on the other side of the Mississippi River. They rested Dusti and Timber in a tree. Their strong arms dropped to their sides. Their wings sagged behind their backs.

Stagnant water pooled across the yards and streets. Dusti flicked his ears as persistent mosquitoes buzzed around him.

People of every race, age, and size were busy piling sandbags around houses. They splashed through puddles of dormant water in thigh-high black booted waders.

Two young men toted sandbags on their shoulders. Their biceps bulged out of their short sleeved shirts as they briskly piled sandbag on top of sandbag around their house.

Next door a wrinkled, frail old lady bit her yellowed fingernails. Her bony, wrinkled arms wrenched a sandbag out of her truck. She lugged it to her house, swaying with every step.

The two young men glanced at the old lady, threw their sandbags on top of their pile only halfway finished, and went over to her house. One man took the sandbag from the lady's feeble arms, while the other began unloading the rest of the sandbags around her house.

Dusti smiled as he watched these two young men love unselfishly. They put their needs to the side without being asked. They had only lived maybe a quarter of their lives, but were willing to help an old neighbor who had already lived most of her life.

"This area has seen many floods," a Lightning Pixie said. "Once, before many of these people's time, the Mississippi River flooded so heavily it made its tributary rivers run backwards. With your help and compassion, Dusti, we will never again see a flood like that."

The old Lightning Pixie flickered over the branches. "We've had a long enough rest. It's time for us to finish our part of the journey."

The Lightning Pixies' wings whirred around Dusti and

Timber. Their tiny fingers wove through Dusti's fur, grabbed his skin, and lifted him into the air.

The Lightning Pixies flew up Arkansas' wild, unabated river. Its untamed torrents tore through the riverbed, rushing to join the mighty Mississippi. Bayous and lakes decorated the northern part of the river.

A canal jutted to the northeast of the Arkansas River. A white tugboat pushing three flat rectangular barges crept up the canal and into the Arkansas River. It prodded the barges westward against the river's current.

The Lightning Pixies flew across the river. Water sprayed Dusti's fur.

Heavy grain fumes wafted from the barges as the Lightning Pixies descended onto them.

"This is where we leave you," the oldest Lightning Pixie said. She tied the small plastic bag around the heart in Dusti's collar. "Ride the barge until it has finished its journey. A way home will find you."

"What about the bag?" Dusti asked. "Where does it go? Who do I give it to?"

The old Lightning Pixie fluttered above Dusti. She tweaked his nose. "The answers will find you along the way. Trust in your heart, Dusti. It will never guide you wrong."

The sun plunged into evening. A dusky crimson illuminated the sky. Cherry, scarlet, and gold splashed across the river. Crickets chirped along the riverbank.

Dusti stared at the river as it slowly faded to black.

"What're you thinking about?" Timber asked rubbing

his back.

Dusti tensed his shoulders and crawled away. "Everything I get close to . . . I lose. I got close to Ryan . . . and I lost him . . . twice."

"You never lost Ryan." Timber pressed her paw against the heart hanging from his collar. "Every time you think of him, he's with you. You still have all the wonderful, precious memories you made together. You can never lose someone you've loved. He'll always be your Ryan and you'll always be his Dusti. Wouldn't you be sad if you had never gotten close to him? It would be like how I feel when you always push me away."

"It's different with you and me. I'd rather you hate me for never . . . getting close to you, instead of pining away for me . . . when I'm gone."

"You're leaving me, Dusti?"

"Not intentionally."

"Not at all. Where you go I go."

"You can't follow me when I . . . die."

"When I die," Timber mocked. "What are you talking about? You won't die."

"Think about it, Tim. The first task takes away . . . my breath. The earth takes away . . . my body. Whatever's in this sack will take away . . . my life. I won't get close to you. Then you can't be sad . . . when I go."

"You're right, Dusti, I wouldn't be sad. I'd be miserable. I'd be sorry I had been through so much with you, but you never considered me a friend. You're planning on leaving, Dusti, not me. It's my choice if I want to get close."

Timber lay against Dusti and wrapped a paw around him. "All I want is to be your friend."

Stars sparkled like diamonds over the river as the barge veered from the left riverbank to the right. Up ahead a thick cement dam stretched across the river while a lock reached downstream on the right side of the riverbank.

The three barges and tugboat slid slowly into the wide, long water filled lock, stopping before a thick metal gate as another metal gate shut behind them. Enormous concrete walls engulfed the sides of the lock like a claustrophobic's nightmare.

Dusti panted. He clambered across the barge looking for a way out.

Timber put a calm paw on him, stopping him in his tracks.

Water poured into the lock.

Dusti nuzzled into Timber waiting for the barges to sink.

The barges and tugboat floated on top of the water as it lifted them to the same level as the river upstream.

A loud horn blast shattered the peaceful night's harmony.

Dusti cuddled into Timber's soft paws as the front metal gate swung open, ending his nightmare. The barges and tugboat floated out of the lock back into the river.

Timber's front paws softly kneaded his tummy. Her unselfish, unwavering, trusting love was unfathomable, but Dusti couldn't help trusting her. He noodgied her frayed orange paws.

That conniving cat. For so long he'd been cautious, never letting anyone in, keeping away from pain and heart-ache. But Timber had found a way to wheedle into his life and then sneak further into his heart.

Dusti cuddled into Timber's stomach. Now with his guard down, he finally felt safe.

CHAPTER THIRTY-TWO
SICK

Dusti hung his paws off the barge, sitting as far away from Timber as he could get. He breathed in the morning air, trying to wrap his head around the feelings darting through his heart.

He never knew he could love someone else as much as he loved Ryan. He thought a love so strong was only meant to be shared with one other mammal. He thought if he were to love anyone else he'd have to divide his love, but it wasn't that way. It was like an additional love grew out of nothing to take in another. How much he could love, now that he knew he'd never have to divide it, was insurmountable.

Dusti crawled over to Timber. He frowned as he looked at her wrapped in a tight ball by the cargo bin.

This quest would have been so much shorter, so much easier to bear if he would've trusted her from the beginning. If she hadn't been so stubborn and stayed by his side even though he insisted on keeping her at leg's length, he would have missed out on a wonderful friend.

Dusti smiled grateful for Timber's hardheaded virtue. He noodgied her cheek.

"Don't touch me," she said curling her head under her paws.

Dusti slunk back to the edge of the barge. His head sank onto his legs as he hung his paws dejectedly over the edge. He deserved that. He had told Timber countless times to get away from him. She probably needed time and space to figure out where they would go from here, how she could annoy him now that he trusted her enough to love her and be her friend.

Bright sunbeams shimmered onto Dusti's paws and beaded across the translucent river as the sun reached past morning into the afternoon. Clear, vibrant water lapsed at the barge's sides, painting rainbows across its wake. Ripples of bass, catfish, and trout swam alongside the barge while it slowly crept up Arkansas' expansive river.

Soft, rolling hills bounded across the riverbanks meshing box elders, red maples, and ash trees together.

A cool breeze blew off the river. Fresh water, fish, and growth perfumed the air almost drowning the thick odor of grain.

Dusti breathed in deeply. He looked at Timber still curled in a ball, waiting, probably, for him to talk first.

"I like this mode of travel . . . best," Dusti said.

Timber held her front paws to her head. "This is the worst for me. I have a pounding headache. Everything's blurry. Sounds get louder by the second."

Timber covered her ears with her paws and buried her nose into her neck.

Dusti nudged her forehead. Heat radiated off her body.

Faint, ghostly stars marked the sky as the barge entered another lock.

Dusti nuzzled Timber's hot head. His flaccid legs crumpled underneath him. He closed his eyes and held his forepaws to his head. Why was Timber sick? She hadn't eaten anything in over a day, but neither had he.

Dusti sniffed around the barge. The sugary smell of grain suffocated the pure night air.

"Tim, wake up," Dusti said shaking Timber. "The grain fumes are . . . making you sick. You need to move . . . away."

Dusti prodded Timber to the edge of the barge.

She lay down, looping her paws over the rim. Her whiskers quivered as the fresh river breeze tickled against her face. "What if I fall into the river?"

"You won't. I'm right next to you. I'll keep you safe. I promise."

A loud grating noise woke Dusti from a troubled sleep. A lock's heavy metal gate jarred open before the barges. A lurid horn blast broke the tranquility of morning.

Timber covered her ears.

"Are you feeling any . . . better?" Dusti asked rubbing her back.

Timber shrank away from Dusti and dug her paws into her forehead. "Get away from me. My head's pounding and everything's so loud."

Dusti slid his paws away from Timber as the barge merged into a lake on the other side of the lock.

The lucid water had turned an opaque gray as the sun hid behind overcast clouds.

Fierce wind beat against the barge rocking it back and forth. It pelted Timber's ears against her head.

Maple trees shuddered across the lake's shore as thunder trembled across the earth. Murky fog swallowed the dim glow of sun. Dark forest shadows reeled from the northern Boston Mountains.

Dusti jumped as a terrifying boom of thunder shook the barge.

Rain barreled onto the lake.

The interlacing raindrops made visibility impossible. The tugboat coaxed the barges close to the shore and moored them there.

Dusti dodged through the rain to Timber. Her drenched orange fur looked like a soggy sandwich. Her whiskers sagged to her chin. She covered her ears and squeezed her eyes shut as the thunder and lightning reverberated into the darkness.

Dusti threw his body on top of hers. "No complaints, Tim. The rain will make you . . . even sicker. You need body heat. I'll keep you dry."

Dusti sheltered Timber as the rain beat in a heavy downpour for hours. Rain dripped from his whiskers and puddled on his shoulders. The cold wetness drizzled into his bones.

*   *   *

Thick, gray fog wrapped around the afternoon sun as a light rain sprinkled onto the lake of emaciated mud. The tugboat slipped the barges into the muddy lake water, pushing them along their journey again.

A loud screech ripped across the muddy water. A bald eagle dove into the lake, his long talons skimming across the muddy surface. His broad brown wings lengthened as he rose into the air empty taloned. His cold, black eyes scrutinized the barge, falling on Dusti.

Dusti's legs shook as he stood protectively over Timber.

The eagle soared toward the barge, dropping lower the closer he got. His cold black eyes dissected Dusti.

Dusti glowered. He hissed loudly.

The eagle circled. He snapped his beak and shot back into the air.

Dusti slumped onto Timber, nudging her awake. "How are you feeling?"

"My throat is sore," Timber whispered in a coarse mew. Her stomach muscles contracted. A low deep throated cough burst from her mouth. "The cold is digging into my bones. My head doesn't hurt anymore, though, but I am hungry."

"I can't do anything about . . . the food. I can warm you up." He brushed his long pink tongue over Timber's head. He dragged it through her tangled, damp fur.

A dark starless sky impeded the night. A feeble purr mumbled from Timber's nose as she fell asleep in Dusti's paws.

CHAPTER THIRTY-THREE
LOSS

The bright yellow sun reached high into the central sky as the barges squeezed through another lock. A steady flutelike whistle harmonized with a soft breeze blowing through the elm, hickory, and pine trees. Fluent rolling hills bounded along the river.

Dusti and Timber stretched on the edge of the barge. The warm sun saturated into their fur, skin, and bones. It shimmered on the hazy water as the mud slowly settled back to the bottom of the river.

Timber's stomach growled.

Dusti looked around the barge and river trying to find anything to pacify her hunger.

A stream of brown feathered wings descended in front of the boat.

"Don't move," Dusti said. "An eagle wants to . . . turn us into lunch."

Eight flutelike notes buzzed through the air.

Timber squinted into the sky. "That's a meadowlark, not an eagle."

A bright yellow breasted meadowlark hopped onto the barge.

Dusti skulked toward the bird, scraping his belly against the barge's rough wood surface.

The meadowlark sang as his short yellow legs skipped around the cargo bin. "I find grain for me to eat, on the plains or in these fleets. I find grain it does sustain, on the barge or in the plains."

The meadowlark hopped from his stash of grain into Dusti's smiling face.

"AHHH," he squealed. He flashed his white tail feathers and threw his wings out to his side. "I knew my time would come someday. Make it quick, laddie."

The meadowlark fell across the barge in a mock faint. "Hopefully, my wife, children, ma, and pa can survive without me." He threw his wing across his forehead and sighed.

Dusti prodded the meadowlark up. "I won't eat you. We're friends."

"Herbivores are not friends with carnivores. All of that meat eating gets in the way. Unless . . ."

The meadowlark hopped around Dusti. He waved his wing beside his head. "Lands sakes alive, we are friends. Wow, nobody will believe this. Where's the orange cat?"

"How do you know me?" Dusti asked.

"Every meadowlark knows about the cat with the crooked tail and his little orange friend. You two saved a baby and mamma in Nebraska. You're where legends come from."

Dusti shrugged.

"So what do you need? You can ask lil' Larky for anything and I'll get it for you."

"Can you get us . . . some food?"

Water splashed ahead of the barge. The bald eagle ricocheted out of the river with a huge largemouth bass in his curved talons. The fish writhed in the eagles grasp.

"I can't catch things like that," the meadowlark said. "My legs don't work that way."

"Could you ask the eagle . . . to share?"

The meadowlark twittered a low note. "They said you were smart, but that's the dumbest thing I've ever heard. I'm not going near that eagle. He'd tear apart lil', ol' me and probably you, too. Any smart bird or cat knows to stay away from eagles."

The meadowlark stared into the filmy river. "I'll try to catch you something. It won't be as big as what the eagle caught."

The meadowlark flew by the shore. His thin brownish black wings glided adjacent to the river. He dipped his yellow beak into the water, flew back to the barge, and spit out a minnow.

"There you go, me lady," he said tipping his beak. "One little minnow won't be enough for you." He soared to the shoreline again and again.

An abundant pile of minnows flopped back and forth in front of Dusti and Timber as the meadowlark threw one more minnow on the pile.

Dusti rested his paw on the meadowlark's tail feathers.

"Thank you. That's plenty. We don't need . . . anymore."

The meadowlark pulled his tail feathers away from
Dusti's grasp. "It's time lil' Larky leaves before you decide you want a full course meal rather than just fish appe-
tizers. I bid you two adieus."

The meadowlark jumped into the air and soared above
the barge.

"Thanks for the food," Dusti and Timber yelled after the
meadowlark.

"Anytime, glad I could help a couple of heroes, even if
they are cats."

The small minnows flopped in front of Dusti as he waited for Timber to eat as many as she could handle. He
licked his jowls as the fresh algae smell of fish teased his
nostrils.

Timber passed some minnows to Dusti. He wolfed
them down; only savoring the watery, oily after taste they
left in his mouth.

After lunch Dusti and Timber stretched on their sides
and watched the beautiful grass filled prairies roll by the
river. Water saturated above the soil turning the grassland
into a marsh.

A glittering lake transcended the river on the other side
of the lock. An array of people splashed in the lake,
swimming along the shores. A mom and a little toddler girl
cuddled on the beach wrapped in a towel.

Dusti watched the mother and child for as long as possible, taken by their beauty and love. He smiled as he

thought of his quest and where it had taken him so far.

He had seen such a variety of beauty cascading across the land from the mysterious beauty of the Black Hills in South Dakota to the unknown beauty of the plains in Nebraska. He had seen hidden beauty in the forests of Missouri and Mississippi and wild beauty on the river in Arkansas. He had felt and admired the natural beauty and love shared by people and animals.

Dusti held the plastic bag on his collar to his chest. Seeing all the love and beauty made his task and everything he'd been through and lost worthwhile.

Dusti's heart pounded loudly through the bag as if gasping for breath. He looked at his feeble legs and gulped a breath of air. Soon all this beauty and love would be taken from him.

He clenched the bag wanting to tear it away from his chest and throw it into the river.

His paw fell limply away from the bag and thudded on the wooden barge. He had to finish his quest. If he didn't, the beauty and love would be taken away from everyone, not just one cat.

As evening licked the day away, brilliant pink and gold rays chimed across the lake. A deep ruby color swept the sky.

Dusti and Timber nuzzled into each other's paws as a cool night fell across the prairie.

Dusti hugged Timber tightly, cherishing the limited time they still had together.

The barge traveled through locks and dams on the

Arkansas River all night and most of the next day, crossing the Arkansas/Oklahoma state line by early afternoon.

The sun leaned into the western sky as the barge floated into an area of commerce. Tall cylinder silos and masses of long rectangular buildings muddled together on an inlet to the left of the river.

The tugboat pushed the barges almost to the end of the inlet, and moored them on a dock.

"This is where our . . . journey ends," Dusti said. He hopped onto the wooden dock.

"Aye, aye captain," Timber said jumping beside Dusti. "Where do we go now?"

"We've traveled by . . . road, rail, and water. All that's left is . . . air. We should find . . . an airport."

Timber giggled. "We've traveled by air twice already, once with the Pigsie Fairies and then again with the Lightning Pixies. I guess all we have left is our four paws."

"It's going to be a long . . . walk home."

Dusti and Timber ambled through the commerce area, trailing the western sun.

Dusti's legs barely supported his weight. His breath was heavy and deep. Prodding on, he stretched his energy as far as it would go.

A rush of wind exploded out of the sky. A shiny white head glared above as broad brown wings descended over Dusti and Timber.

"Run, Timber!" Dusti yelled. "The eagle!"

Timber streaked back towards the dock. Her body became an orange blaze. Her head sank below her shoulders.

Her tail shot straight behind her body as if it was an arrow pushing her forward.

Dusti scampered after her. His legs couldn't move fast enough. Gasping for breath, he fell into a slow limp.

The bald eagle screeched down. His long, black, curved talons squeezed around Dusti's stomach and shoulders. His broad wings beat against Dusti's body.

Dusti fought vigorously in the eagle's grasp as they soared into the sky, leaving Timber miles and miles away.

CHAPTER THIRTY-FOUR
TORTURE

"I would not fight me," the eagle said. "If I drop you now, you fall to your death." He unclenched Dusti's shoulders.

Dusti's head and shoulders fell through the nothingness of air. He squirmed against the eagle's speed. He pulled the front of his body up, gripping onto anything, but grabbing nothing.

The eagle pulled Dusti's hind end closer to his body. He clasped Dusti's front in his talons again. "Let that be an example of what would happen if you keep fighting me."

Dusti hung limply in the eagles grasp as they flew for days over a medley of land. Oklahoma's thick oak forests banded together on top of sandstone hills, seas of grass ran across the prairie, gypsum hills glittered in the sun as if they were capped with diamonds, and miles of grassland ended in rugged tan mesas.

Black Mesa's flat top cut across the last stretch of Oklahoma. Black lava rocks spotted the mesa as if it had once been a volcano. Stunted juniper trees climbed up the mesa.

The eagle swooped into a rugged niche on the mesa's talus slope. "Wait here," the eagle said, dropping Dusti into the niche. He stretched out his wings and flew into the sky. The sun shimmered on his wings, streaking his brown feathers with a deep gold.

Dusti crawled up the slanted niche. The wind had eroded nooks and holes into the mesa's wall, but they were too far apart for Dusti to use as an escape route. The mesa's sheer wall dropped hundreds of feet below.

A herd of antelope barreled through the short grass stretching across Oklahoma's panhandle as if coming to rescue Dusti by some magical power.

Dusti clenched his paws around the niche's opening and poked his head over. He cried and cried, begging to be rescued.

The antelope bounded toward New Mexico deaf to his cries.

"Please, help me," Dusti screamed. "I'm up here. Please come get me."

A loud yowl answered Dusti's pleadings. A lone bobcat searched the distance from a nearby butte. His sharp canine teeth pricked out of his mouth. His golden coat flashed in the sunset. He prowled his butte freely daring anyone to join him.

Dusti unclenched his paws and slid back into the niche. He growled under his breath. What could he do? He couldn't go anywhere. He couldn't move fast enough to outrun predators. He couldn't catch up with the speeding antelope. He was the eagle's prisoner.

Everything he had done, everything he had been through was for nothing.

He curled his clawless paws under his belly. What was the use of even caring anymore? Everything he loved had been taken away from him. Maybe it was time he stopped fighting. Maybe it was time he gave in.

The plastic bag grew heavy around his neck.

Dusti glanced down. If he gave up now and sacrificed himself to the eagle's bidding, he'd be sacrificing everyone he loved just because he wasn't willing to fight anymore.

He shook his head. He couldn't do that. The eagle could take him away, but Dusti would fight for everyone he loved until he took his very last breath.

Dusti wrapped his front paws around the plastic bag. The eagle didn't get Timber and he would never get the bag. He would protect it with his life until his last task was completed and he was sure everyone he loved was safe.

A powerful gust of wind blasted into the niche. A loud clawing scraped the opening.

The eagle's sharp beak scoffed at Dusti. "You didn't even try to escape?"

"And become an easy target . . . for every predator . . . out there," Dusti said, "not a chance."

An intense screech roared from the eagle's beak. He limped toward Dusti on his clenched claws. "So instead you stay exactly where I put you, waiting for me, a very hungry predator, to return." He snapped his sharp golden beak just above Dusti's head.

"The jokes on you," Dusti said. "You didn't get Timber. She's the one that matters . . . not me."

"Timber, your little orange friend? No. I didn't get her. I left Timber for my friends. They'll do to her exactly what I plan on doing to you."

"What's that?"

"We have many miles to go before I plan on doing anything."

The eagle's shiny black orb eyes glared as a sneering smile traced his beak. "We'll meet up with Timber again."

"Why? So you can torture us . . . together?"

"Some call it torture. I call it survival."

"You can't hurt me."

The eagle glared. He stood to his full height towering over Dusti. He flapped his strong wings. Dust swelled inside the niche.

Dusti gulped for breath. He stood up on his limp legs. "I've lost too much . . . you can't hurt me."

"Enough!" the eagle screeched.

He threw open his talon. A dead mouse skidded across the ground. "Eat."

Dusti pawed the dead mouse. His stomach growled as the sweet scent of fresh meat curled into his nostrils. He greedily tore into the mouse. He needed to keep up his strength until he escaped, saved the United States, and rescued Timber.

The morning glowed burgundy as the eagle and Dusti flew away from the Black Mesa and across Colorado's

Great Plains. Dirt spread across the flatlands with an occasional field of wheat, barley, or hay.

Uncomfortable heat blared from the sun's sharp rays and radiated from the ground. The golden waving wheat cowered in the hot soil. Hay withered in the glare of the sun.

The eagle flew away from the plains and over the Sangre De Cristo Mountains. Stifled shade draped over the dry vegetation ransacking the mountains. Brown pine needles clung to small juniper and piñon trees. Firs and spruce tree's brittle boughs sagged with the weight of pine needles like a withered woman's triceps.

Bright sun rays sprang out of the west as the eagle dove out of the dry forest. He soared over the mountainous sand dunes blooming on the other side of the Sangre De Cristo Mountains.

A staticy sound breezed across the sand dunes as the sand continually shifted from dune to dune.

The eagle gained speed as he flew over the San Luis Valley. The smoky purple San Juan Mountains stretched along the western border like a big banner welcoming Dusti home.

Dusti squirmed in the eagle's grip. If he could escape before he became the eagle's meal, he could find Tippy, find Timber, and then save the United States with their help.

The eagle's talons squeezed tightly around Dusti's stomach. His wings beat roughly through the air gaining altitude.

Clouds of smoke billowed around the top of the San Juan Mountains as if they were an active volcano getting ready to spew.

Heavy, gray haze draped over the mountainside. Smoke intruded the zealous, piney mountain air.

The eagle dodged through the trees as night's dark shadows blurred with the haze. Sinking towards the mountain, the eagle swooped into a jagged cave and dropped Dusti roughly inside.

"Sleep," the eagle said, circling the cave entrance. He hunkered down, curled his head under his wing, and soon was fast asleep.

Dusti licked his fur as thick smoky air billowed into the cave.

He gagged and glared at the cave's opening. The eagle's large body guarded the cave entrance, not letting anyone out or in.

Dusti's mind raced throughout the night. How could he find Tippy, find Timber, and finish his task with this great feathery oaf wasting his time? He couldn't escape. The only way out of this mess was to ask the eagle for help.

As the first rays of sun tickled the fir and juniper trees the eagle woke, stretching out his broad wings and rolling his head around his neck. His orb eyes glowered. A mocking frown scoffed across his beak.

"Please," Dusti begged. "Let me go. I have to finish . . . my quest."

"Quest?"

"Yes. I have to save the . . . United States."

"Saving the USA are you? And what exactly have you done?"

"I gave the north wind. I gave the southeast earth. Please, I need to give the west. . . what it needs."

"What does the west need?"

"I don't know. I need your help. Please, help me before . . . we're destroyed."

"The United States is already destroyed. Floods and tornadoes ravage the south, east, and north. And let me show you what's happening to the west."

The eagle's talons wrenched around Dusti pulling him out of the cave.

Thick smoke clouded the sky.

Dusti gulped the heavy air.

Scorched forests charred the mountain. Smoke billowed from the treetops. Burned meat loitered in the air. A raging inferno gulped bushes, trees, houses and anything in the way. Red, dancing flames jumped from tree to tree.

"That doesn't look like saving to me," the eagle said. "You're destroying the USA."

"No, I'm saving it. It just isn't balanced, yet."

"Fire ravages the dry land. There's nothing you can do to save us."

"Yes, there is." Dusti rolled in the eagle's talons. He grabbed the plastic bag in his teeth and ripped it open. "The west needs water. I'm here to give it some."

One lonely drop of water dribbled out as Dusti overturned the bag.

The blood drained from Dusti's face. His head throbbed. A searing hot pain pounded against his skull. His blood boiled through his body as if life was draining out of him.

Blackness teemed across the sky. Rain flooded the land.

The eagle flapped his wings against the pounding rain.

Dusti flopped lifelessly in the eagle's talons as his world went dark.

CHAPTER THIRTY-FIVE
TARNISHED

Wind pounded through the valley, leaving a dank, charred smell in its wake.

Shards of pine trees dotted the San Juan Mountains. Bare pine limbs clung to blackened stems.

Wet ash stuck to a pea green house's rooftop as if it had snowed. Gray, murky water dripped from the house's gables.

Steam rose from a pool bubbling out of the ground.

Fire had tainted the wind, earth, and water.

The soft, warm ground cradled around Dusti as his chest wheezed fighting for air. His breath rasped in his throat. His legs shook uncontrollably as a spasm ran through his body. A throbbing pain hammered against his skull. With great effort he squeezed his eyes shut, closing out the miserable world. All he had done, all he had been through, all that he lost was for this.

An emblazoned screech tore through the sky.

Dusti wrenched open his eyes.

Mighty brown wings beat against the wind. A bald eagle soared underneath a double rainbow arcing its prismatic colors across the San Juan Mountains.

Timber. He had to find Timber.

Dusti lifted his heavy body onto his limp paws. He took a step.

The eagle and rainbow blurred into a brown blob. Dusti's head rolled flaccidly around his collared neck. His legs collapsed under him.

Claws clenched his shoulder. "Dusti."

He blinked. Fluffy whiteness danced in front of him. He shut his eyes and then slowly opened them, registering on two bright blue eyes.

"Tippy," Dusti whispered.

"You have come back to me," Tippy said. His white paw brushed Dusti's cheek. "It took you a while to come around, but you returned like you promised."

"Tippy," Dusti panted. "She risked her life . . . for me. I couldn't get her back." He wheezed and sucked in air. Tears swelled out of his eyes. "I have to get her, Tippy. I love her."

"Who?" Tippy asked.

"Timber."

A wet noodgie pelted against Dusti's cheek. A tattered orange paw covered his mouth. "Don't talk, Dusti," Timber said. "Save your strength."

"But," he inhaled, "the eagles."

"The eagles came to help you," Tippy said. "It's hard for such a majestic animal to admit he's helping a cat.

Their nature is to hunt smaller animals, not nurture them."

"Vultures would've been better," Timber said.

Tippy's face glowed like fire. "Timber and Dusti, because of you the United States is saved."

"No," Dusti said. He swallowed the air, choking on the feeble amount he could seep into his lungs. "Disasters have destroyed . . . the United States. We couldn't save it."

"Disasters have damaged the United States, not destroyed it," Tippy said. "The powerful wind in the north has turned into a whisper spreading pollen and seeds. The churning water in the southeast recedes leaving rich, fertile soil. Here the fire has unlocked nutrients into the soil that were hidden in dead decaying trees. The north, south, east, and west will soon have new growth, rebuilding a new and better earth that could have never existed if you hadn't saved it."

"Then let me die," Dusti panted. "I did everything . . . I could. Timber's safe. The United States is . . . saved. I have nothing . . . left . . . to give." He sucked in a deep breath. The air withered out of his body before reaching his lungs. His head flopped to the side. His blood pooled at the tips of his paws.

Timber rubbed Dusti's quivering back. "Tippy, do something."

"It would be a pity," Tippy said, "to give up now after everything you've been through, everything you've done. You've sacrificed your blood, body, and breath, but you haven't given everything, you still have one thing left."

"I can't fight . . . anymore." Dusti inhaled deeply. "I

don't have it . . . in me." His heart slowed as if squeezing out the last drop of blood.

A sharp bite pinched the nape of Dusti's neck. His body rubbed against the wet dirt as Tippy and Timber dragged him to the pool of steaming water. The smell of sulfur beaded the air.

"Phosphate, iron, zinc, and other minerals abound," Tippy said, "where living waters bubble from the ground. Immerse Dusti in the water, Timber, before death rings his toll."

Fiery, hot water washed over Dusti. He sank to the bottom of the pool. The earth burned against his paws. A smoldering spring rippled from the bottom of the pool as if pushed by the wind.

Fire kindled around him. It had infiltrated the earth, water, and wind. Fire—the one thing Dusti didn't give the United States.

Water crushed Dusti's head and lungs. He struggled to the top of the pool, thrashing against the weighty water. He lifted his head above the surface, gasping for breath.

"What one thing do you have left, Dusti?" Tippy asked.

"My fire, my soul."

Dusti plummeted to the bottom of the pool. The heart on his collar thudded on his chest.

Warm water saturated his body. Blood coursed through his veins. Water and minerals seeped into his skin, firming his muscles and solidifying his bones.

The spring's gentle waves kneaded the aches out of his body. Tepid water enfolded around him like Ryan's hands.

Euphoria pulsed through him as the balmy earth cushioned his tired body. All he had done, all he had been through, and now he could finally sleep.

"No," Dusti said. He wrestled against the luring water. He beat his paws against the burning earth. He shot his head through the water, breaking the surface, and gulped the sweet vapory air. A mass of oxygen twirled around his lungs.

Timber's white whiskers twitched on her pale orange face. Tears glistened in the corner of her green eyes. Her frayed orange paws gripped the rough rocks around the pool. Tippy patted her bowed head.

Dusti paddled through the water. He noodgied Timber's heart shaped nose. "I'm okay, Timber. The pool healed everything broken on me."

Tears dropped like dew onto Timber's whiskers. "I thought you died, Dusti. Tippy wouldn't let me go in and save you. I thought you had left me for good."

"I would never leave you," Dusti said.

The damp earth squished between Dusti's pads as he hopped out of the pool. The sun glittered through the valley, casting a vibrant rainbow across the two mountain ranges. It sparkled on the heart around Dusti's neck. A newborn smell of green growth whispered from the ground. The pool gurgled as water poured from the spring.

"I had to go to the bottom again," Dusti said. "The pool saved my life."

"You saved your own life," Tippy said. He ran around the pool. "The pool only helps heal unnecessary imperfections. You're the one who fought the water to reclaim your breath. You're the one who has vanquished death." He jumped in the air, looped his forelegs around his hind legs, and cannonballed into the pool. His body melted into the steam, vanishing before it splashed into the water.

Dusti flexed his clawless forepaws around the pool and stared into the clear water. His bottom jaw kinked to the left of his upper jaw. He erected his spiraled tail.

Timber rubbed Dusti's back. "Tippy's not in the pool. He vanished like the other times."

"I know, but Tippy wanted me to see myself." He breathed in. His blood rushed through his body. He stood on sturdy legs. He wagged his erected, spiraled tail. "The pool didn't take away the imperfections that make me who I am." He smiled. His bottom snaggletooth gleamed on his upper lip. "I'm back to the tarnished, loveable kitten I've always been."

"Loveable?" Timber batted Dusti's ear. Her green eyes sparkled like emeralds. "I'm glad something could make you loveable, I never could."

Dusti tackled Timber onto the soft mushy ground. "Be nice or you can't come with me."

"Where do you plan on going?" Timber asked. "To a black willow or an eagles nest, no wait we've already been there, haven't we? What could be worse than an eagle?"

"I have a better place this time, a real home and a real family who will love us."

Dusti led Timber across the damp dirt to the pea green house. A diesel and sulfur smell lingered in the wind. Two kids, a rough brown haired boy and a curlicued blonde haired girl, played in the front yard of the gable roofed house. A maroon semi sat on a long dirt driveway.

"Tom's house!" Timber exclaimed.

"I know I didn't trust him," Dusti said, "but a wiser cat convinced me otherwise."

"I'm glad you've finally come around. Listening to me will make your life much easier."

Timber shot down the driveway. She brushed against the children's legs. "Meow, meow."

Dusti slipped up the three whitewashed steps. A piney smell of soap, aftershave, and deodorant spilled off the porch. A curly, blonde haired man rocked back and forth on the front porch swing. His tan arm flipped the thin pages of a cow magazine he was reading.

"Meow," Dusti said.

Tom put down the magazine. He inched his pointer finger toward Dusti. "Here kitty, kitty."

Dusti hopped into his lap. He slid his scent glands across Tom's hand.

The curlicued girl carried Timber up the steps. She smiled at her dad and rocked the mangled, orange furred cat in her chubby arms.

Timber's long orange tail curled around the girl's wrist. Her ears squashed to the side as the brown haired boy rubbed her head. A loud purr belted out of her nose.

Tom fingered the collar hanging around Dusti's neck. He held the heart. A great laugh boomed out of his mouth, shaking the swing back and forth.

Toothy, enchanted smiles lit the children's faces. Two deep dimples dug into the girl's round cheeks as a crooked mischievous smile slid up the right side of the boy's face.

Tom dug a phone out of his pocket and dialed a number. "Ryan," he said. He patted the cats' heads as if christening them and said, "Timber and Dusti."

A loud happy squeal rang from the phone.

EPILOGUE

Green cascaded over the earth. Piñon, juniper, aspen, fir, and spruce trees covered the mountains. The wind glided through the valley carrying the smell of pine, dirt, green, and growth. Crystal clear remnants of rain dribbled from the gables of the pea green house.

A maroon semi roared down the driveway as the sun tinted the garnet sky with flares of gold.

After the semi stopped, a skinny, orange cat pelted out of the driver's door and ran across the driveway. Her long orange tail stood tall, the tip swishing back and forth. A silver heart medallion hung from her collar and thudded on her chest.

Dusti slid down the maple tree he had climbed. He flew down the driveway and noodgied Timber. "How was the trip," he asked, licking sunflower dust off Timber's head.

"Like always, great," Timber said. "Growth thrives everywhere. Wheat and grass flourish across the plains, fruits are blossoming from the trees, and vegetables are peeking from the ground. I love seeing the United States' diverse beauty from the road. You should really think about coming with us. Traveling is so peaceful."

"Thought about it, have done it, never want to do it again," Dusti said. "Besides, I need to stay and protect Tom's wife and kids while he's gone."

"Of course." Timber noodgied Dusti's cheek. "We brought someone back with us."

A tall teenage boy careened out of the semi holding a blue suitcase. His big hands feathered his curly, honey-blonde hair across his forehead. He walked to the front porch and sat down next to Tom on the swing.

The family horded on the porch and sat captivated as Tom recounted another journey from the road.

Timber climbed into Tom's lap, making his story lapse for a minute or two while she became the center of attention.

As the story resumed Timber cuddled into Tom's lap. A rich purr hummed from her throat, adding cadence to Tom's lyrical tale.

Ryan's lean face lit up as he listened to Tom's story. His straight grown-up teeth twinkled in a huge smile. A manly, deep laugh rumbled from his mouth.

Dusti's life had become better than great ever since the quest. Ryan, Timber, Tom and his family loved him unselfishly and unconditionally. Ryan got to visit twice every year, once in the summer by himself and then again at Christmas with his mom and Shane.

"Dusti," Ryan called, "here kitty, kitty." His baby blue eyes twinkled.

Dusti charged onto the porch and jumped into Ryan's lap. He kneaded Ryan's blue jeans as Ryan's rough worked hands stroked his throat underneath his crooked jaw. Ryan was growing into a great young man any cat would be proud of.

Dusti stood up, climbed Ryan's chest, and noodgied his nose. He circled Ryan's lap, wagging his perfectly twisted, perfectly wretched tail.

THANK YOU

I'd like to send a big thank you first to everyone who has read this book. Thank you so much for supporting me and giving me your time.

Next I'd like to thank the people that helped in my research: Cody Hulet, Jaime Valdez, Donny Henson, and Bob Harris. Thank you for answering my questions about semis, trucking, trains, and river locks. Without you guys I would have been extremely lost. If I misrepresented trucking, trains, and river locks, in any way it is from my lack of understanding.

I am very grateful for all of the librarians, libraries, extension offices, and different counties' chambers of commerce that gave me information. Thank you all for making my novel more complete.

THANK YOU

THANK YOU

Thank you to my friends and family, both immediate and extended. Thank you for believing in me and pushing me until I succeed.

I would like to finish with a great big THANK YOU to my family Alex, Kelti, and Ayden. Thank you for supporting my dreams, believing in me, and listening to me on road trips read revision after revision of my novel. I'm the luckiest wife and mom in the whole wide world!

THANK YOU

If I've offended any cats, goats, pronghorns, turtles, armadillos, or any species of bird in any way, please forgive me that was not my intention.

If you'd like more information about me,
Sari Ann Koehler, or the books I have written
my web address is: www.sariannkoehler.com

Dear Readers,

Thank you for reading my book. I hope while you read it you were able to explore some of the wonders of the United States of America through my eyes. More importantly, I hope it filled you with enough curiosity that you will want to explore and discover new parts of the United States of America for yourself. Wherever you may go, and whatever you may do, I hope it's something exciting, beautiful, and new.

Until next time-

Sari A. Koehler